RETURN TO THE PAINTED CAVE

RETURN
TO THE
PAINTED CAVE

JUSTIN DENZEL

PHILOMEL BOOKS · NEW YORK

Library of Congress Cataloging-in-Publication Data
Denzel, Justin F. Return to the painted cave / Justin Denzel.
p. cm.   Summary: Fourteen-year-old Tao, a cave painter living
in prehistoric times, sets out on an odyssey to bring healing
to the blind girl, Deha, and the outcast children.
[1. Cave paintings—Fiction. 2. Man, Prehistoric—Fiction.]
I. Title. PZ7.D4377Re 1997 [Fic]—dc20 96-21127 CIP AC
ISBN 0-399-23117-X 10 9 8 7 6 5 4 3 2 1
First Impression

To Ken and Elsie,
for all their bits and bytes

RETURN TO THE PAINTED CAVE

Prologue

Lightning flashed down from the towering black clouds, and the earth shook with thunder.

Zugor, the mad shaman, stood in the clearing, surrounded by the elders and the people of the mountain clan. His mass of grizzly hair flew out around him, swept by the wind-driven rain.

The clan people cowered before him, eyes wide with fright.

A twelve-year-old girl stood near the madman, staring blankly into space as if in a trance. She held a small deformed child in her arms, while two other misshapen children stood beside her, cold and shivering, their arms wrapped around her legs.

"Hear me, people of the mountain clan," the madman screeched. "Graybeard is gone, and I come to rid you of the curse of evil that hangs over your camp." He motioned to the girl and the three children. "You give shelter to this blind girl possessed of demons and to these orphans of evil." He hissed as he spoke. "So now I take them away to a cave in the mountains, away from the light of day, to a place where their demons will not touch the people or taint the land."

Rutar, the leader of the clan, stepped forward and asked in a gruff voice, "By whose summons do you come to take Graybeard's place?"

The mad shaman glared at him and pointed a bony finger in his face. "By the voices of the mountain spirits," he sneered. "Mark my words and do as I say, or I will put a curse of doom on this camp."

Just then a flash of lightning struck the old oak tree in the valley, sending it crashing to the ground.

Zugor laughed. "You see, you see that? There is the power of my magic!"

The elders fell back behind their leader, trembling.

"Do not anger him," one of them said. "If he wants to take the blind girl and the children, let him."

The people nodded and moved back.

Rutar shrugged. "We have seen the fire from the sky many times before. It is no different now."

Another elder spoke up. "But it is well that we do his bidding. We have troubles enough. We want no curses or spells."

An old woman moved out from the crowd. She put her arm around the orphans. "These children have done nothing. If they be banished, I will take care of them."

The leader shook his head, still uncertain.

Thunder rumbled from above, mixing with the madman's laughter. "Do not tempt the spirits!" he shouted.

Rutar searched the faces of his elders. Their eyes showed fear. "Then let it be so," he said. "The blind girl and children will go with Zugor."

1

Tao stood on the high cliffs and looked out over the open grasslands. Far in the distance, a half-day's journey away, he could make out the line of purple hills that was the Land of the Mountain People. He had not been there since Graybeard's death more than two years ago, but tomorrow night he would paint images of the great beasts in the Secret Cavern to bring good luck with the hunting.

The Mountain People lived a hard life in the rugged hill country, gathering edible roots, tubers, and mushrooms in the dark forests; hunting ibex and mountain sheep high among the rocky crags. When game was scarce they often raided the bison herds down in the grasslands beyond the river, an offense that angered the Valley People. For this reason, and because he was a member of the Valley clan, Tao knew his visit could be risky.

Carrying a skin pouch filled with chalks, sketch stones, and flints, Tao hobbled out across the open plains. Born with a twisted foot, he had learned to overcome the disability by curving his leg around the shaft of his spear and vaulting over the ground. In this way he could travel as far and as fast as a grown man.

Tao glanced up to see the stars come out one by one, flickering across the sky. He hurried along, for he wanted to be in the mountains by early morning in order to have a full day's rest before the sacred rituals.

His wolf dog, Ram, loped ahead of him, pushing through the tufts of tall bunchgrass, flushing up coveys of quail and ground doves.

A tawny owl swooped past Tao's face so close that he felt the breath of its wings across his cheek. He sniffed the sweet fragrance of the new bunchgrass, and he knew that spring was not far away. Soon great herds of bison and antelope would move through the valley. Later, maybe even the great mammoths would come.

A big yellow moon climbed into the sky, bathing the grasslands in a pale glow of light. A nightjar flew up at Tao's feet, scolding in its shrill *churit, churit.*

All at once the wolf dog's body stiffened. Tao looked up quickly. Not far off, in the dim light, he saw a small band of horses silhouetted against the horizon. They were early arrivals, and Tao knew Ram had caught their scent.

Tao reached down and put a collar around the wolf
dog's neck. It was one Kala, his foster mother, had made
for him from the skin of a summer fawn. Then he tied
a strong cedar-root leash to the collar and held tightly
as the wolf dog strained to give chase.

Tao watched the horses for a moment before going
on. He hoped they would stay in the valley long enough
so he might study them and etch their images on one
of his slate stones.

Ram's yellow slitted eyes gleamed in the hazy moonlight. His head reached up to Tao's waist. The thick fur
around his neck and shoulders shimmered a silvery
gray. He pulled against the leash, his breath catching in
his throat, eager to be on the chase. It took all of Tao's
strength to hold the wolf dog back.

A night breeze blew from the other side of the valley,
and Tao knew the horses had not yet picked up their
scent. He walked steadily, his deerskin boots rustling
through the damp grass.

All at once Ram stopped. He turned back, growling.
Tao almost stumbled over him. He glanced around
quickly to see what had caught Ram's attention.

At first he saw only the dancing shadows of the scattered birch trees. Then he winced. Not far away, over
the tops of the waist-high grass, he saw the head of a
huge cave lion.

Tao held Ram tightly, keeping him close against his

leg. In his haste to reach the mountains, the boy had taken a shortcut, crossing the plains at night when the lions were on the hunt. This big one was well known to all the nearby clan people. They called him Sandar. Tonight he and his pride were after the horses, and Tao was in his way.

Even now Tao saw the angry beast staring at him. Then the head disappeared and Tao saw the grass sway as Sandar moved closer. He heard soft rustling sounds, and he knew Sandar's pride of hungry females was creeping up all around them.

Ram growled and tugged at the leash. Tao pulled hard to hold him back. "Stay," he whispered. "You are strong but no match for a cave lion."

Tao looked back and saw Sandar only a stone's throw away. Yellow moonlight glinted in his dark brown eyes. His great shoulders bulged like a huge panther's.

The boy stood quietly, spellbound by the savage beauty, the great shaggy head, the rippling lines of the massive body. In spite of the approaching danger, he stopped for a moment and wished he could paint Sandar on the wall of a Secret Cavern. He remembered how he had sat on the edge of the cliff last summer and sketched Sandar's image on one of his slate stones. But never had he seen the great lion so close.

His thoughts were interrupted by a snarling growl as Sandar crept up. Quickly Tao moved to one side, pulling Ram after him. Sandar followed, crouching, stalking.

Again Ram pulled at the leash.

Tao glanced around, trying to think of something to do. By force of habit, he reached into his leather pouch and felt the cold smoothness of the shining stone given to him by the old shaman Graybeard. With it he could aim a flash of light in an animal's eyes and drive it off. It had saved his life more than once, but it would work only in bright sunlight, not at night.

He withdrew his hand and waited as Sandar appeared again, so close he could hear the low rumble of his breathing. He could also hear the pride of females moving in, tightening the circle. He wanted to run but he knew it would only excite the lions and bring them roaring down upon him.

Tao heard the soft whinny of the horses. He peered across the plains to see them still shadowed against the horizon. They galloped back and forth, tossing their heads, sniffing the air, and Tao was sure they too sensed the closeness of the lions.

He watched them for a moment as they crowded into one another, milling about, uncertain. Then he glanced down at Ram. The wolf dog stared back at Sandar, snarling.

Once again Tao looked off at the horses. Then he dropped his spear. Quickly he started to untie the leash on Ram's collar. His hands trembled; his fingers slipped on the cedar-bark cord. He heard the grass rustle behind him as Sandar crept closer, a low growl coming from deep in his throat.

Sweat covered the back of Tao's neck. The palms of his hands felt cold and wet. His fingers, still slipping, fumbled with the tangled knot around Ram's collar. It seemed to take forever. Then it came loose. Tao reached down. He grabbed the wolf dog's head in both hands and faced him out across the plains, directing Ram's eyes toward the horizon. He knew the wolf could not see through the tall grass. But he could smell. "Ram," he whispered, "horses." He felt Ram's body tense. He reached up with his right hand and pointed to show the way. "Go," he said, "chase the horses."

Ram leaped forward, plunging through the grass, heading directly for the milling herd of horses. Tao knew he would circle around behind them and drive them toward him.

Then Tao picked up his spear and turned to face Sandar. The lion's dark eyes bore into him. The boy waited. His hands trembled. He jammed the butt end of his spear into the ground and held it out in front of him the way he had seen Graybeard do, hoping Sandar would leap upon it and impale himself on the sharp point.

Then he braced himself and stood in the tall grass,

breathing hard, waiting for the lion to come on. For a moment the moon disappeared behind a cloud. A purple darkness settled over the plains. Tao stared into the night. He listened for the crashing sound of a charging lion, but only the strident trill of the early spring toads broke the silence. Sandar seemed to have vanished.

Tao felt his heart pound. He stood firmly behind his spear, trying to hold it steady. A moment later the moon came out from behind the clouds. He saw Sandar creeping up on him, a great tawny shadow, his head level with his own. For a moment the lion's huge bulk filled his vision.

Sandar snorted, and his warm breath steamed on the cool night air. But instead of leaping he came through the grass in a slow loping trot, as if he knew the boy could not escape.

Quickly Tao picked up his spear and backed away, the tough grasses whipping across the backs of his legs.

Sandar followed. He came on deliberately, in a straight line.

Tao reached back and threw the spear with all his might. Sandar reared up and slapped it to the ground as if it were a twig. With a snarling growl he pounced.

Tao stumbled backward to get out of the way, but his foot caught in a badger hole. He spun around and fell to the ground. He lay there, panting heavily as the big cat stood over him.

Sandar leaned down, a white froth dripping from his muzzle. His black lips curled up, and Tao saw the long white fangs glisten in the moonlight as the beast made ready to strike.

In a futile gesture, Tao threw his hands up over his face.

Then, over the low droning chorus of night sounds, Tao heard the thunder of pounding hooves.

Sandar heard it too. He lifted his head, sniffing the air. His great body stiffened, and he stood there, tense and uncertain.

The galloping hooves shook the earth as the horses thundered across the plains, and Tao knew Ram was driving them on.

Sandar held his head up, waiting. A moment later the stampeding horses rushed in. They raced by in head-long panic. One came straight for Tao. It did not see him lying in the grass. At the last moment it saw the lion. With a screeching whinny it swerved to one side, its legs flying, its hooves tearing up the sod.

Sandar spun around, leaping up at the passing horse, clawing at its rump, hanging on as the frightened ani-mal plunged into the grass.

Tao jumped to his feet, horses pounding all around him, swerving, squealing in panic. He shouted and swung his arms about to wave them off. Some passed so close he could feel the swish of their tails.

They galloped off in all directions, and the boy could

hear the shrieking screams of the ones pulled down by the female lions.

Then, save for the echoing roar of Sandar a short distance away, all was quiet.

2

With his knees still shaking, Tao picked up his spear and hobbled on across the valley. He crossed a shallow brook and came to a grove of willows. There Ram jumped out, his tail wagging. Tao leaned down and threw his arms around him.

They rested awhile. Then Tao tied the root leash to Ram's collar, and they continued on across the plains. They walked all night, skirting around scattered groves of birch trees and alders growing along the streams. Twice they flushed up small bands of red deer that were bedded down for the night, frightening them off into the darkness.

It was almost dawn when they reached the river. There Tao found his little raft of pine logs that he had made last summer, still beached in a low thicket of willow bushes where he had left it.

A night heron, perched on top of it, flapped off with an angry squawk as Tao and Ram climbed aboard. Tao pushed it out into the stream and poled the little craft with the butt end of his spear.

Long strings of graylag geese flew low overhead, honking as they greeted the rising sun. Now and then a glistening pike leaped out of the water, snapping at a darting mayfly or water bug.

The shoaling waters gurgled and swirled around them, and they soon reached the opposite shore, where Tao pulled the raft up on the shingle beach. He looked up into the high hills and saw the hazy white smoke hanging in the treetops as it rose up from the early morning cook fires of the Mountain People.

Tao held Ram on the leash as they climbed up the steep slope through the thick forest of spruce trees. In some places the ground leveled off, then rose up again until it reached the base of the mountain. There the gray rocky walls towered over them. Clumps of stunted pine trees grew out of the cracks and crevices. Patches of green and yellow lichen covered the walls as high as Tao could see.

They walked along the foot of the cliffs with Ram darting from side to side, sniffing along the trail. He whined softly as he pulled at the leash, and Tao knew he was picking up the scent of strangers. He held him close now, expecting at any moment to run into a band of clan hunters.

Once a soft rain of pebbles tumbled down the rocky wall. Tao glanced up quickly, his eyes searching the high jagged rocks. But it was only a young ibex leaping from ledge to ledge.

Then Ram stopped short to sniff around a slate stone lying by the side of the trail. Tao yanked on the leash, but the wolf dog pulled back, refusing to leave the stone. He nudged it with his nose, pushing it across the ground.

Tao reached down and picked it up. It was flat and oval-shaped, larger than a man's hand. He glanced at it quickly and was about to throw it away, when he turned it over. He blinked and gasped. There, on the opposite side, was a beautiful engraving of a running horse. The lines were etched into the gray slate stone with painstaking care and accuracy. The magnificent head sat upon an arched neck poised on strong, muscular shoulders. The graceful body raced in full gallop and had a long flowing tail.

Tao studied it closely for a while, admiring the skill and craftsmanship. As an artist he had painted in the caves of his own people and of those of the River and Lake clans. But he had yet to see anything as fine and detailed as this. He was sure it was not the work of Graybeard, though it showed some of the same tricks of hand. But he knew that whoever had carved this engraving was a master artist, a skilled maker of images.

He wrapped the slate carefully in a handful of soft fern leaves and placed it in his leather pouch along with his other sketch stones.

He tugged gently on Ram's leash, and they started out again. They had gone only a short way when Tao heard the lilting sound of a flute. The melodic notes drifted on the morning air. He glanced up to where splashes of sunlight played across the face of the gray cliffs. There he could make out the dark opening of a little cave. Tao stood, staring up at it, certain that it must be the source of the music.

He lingered awhile, smiling as he listened to the joyous notes. Then he went on his way, wondering who was the musician of the flute and who was the artist of the beautiful engraving. Were they, perhaps, one and the same?

Now Tao and Ram made their way down a path leading through a thick growth of ferns and laurel bushes, toward the camp of the Mountain People.

Halfway down, Ram stopped, the hair along the ridge of his back bristling. Tao held him back, waiting.

A moment later the laurel bushes parted, and four armed men stepped out of the shadows. They wore breechcloths of bearskin and wolverine fur. They pressed around Tao, pointing their spears at his chest and back, their eyes narrowed, full of suspicion.

"You hunt on our land," one of the men growled. "Why? What clan do you come from?" He was a big man, wearing a mouflon robe and a necklace of bear claws. He scowled down at Tao as he tugged at his wiry black beard.

The boy shook his head. "I am Tao of the Valley People. The spring hunting is about to begin, and I come to paint images of the great beasts in your Secret Cavern."

The man laughed, a rough, taunting laugh. He pointed at Ram. "You bring a wolf dog for this? I think you lie. Maybe you come to hunt our ibex or mouflon, eh?"

Ram growled and bared his fangs. Tao strained to hold him back. "I do not hunt your mouflon or ibex," Tao said quietly. "There is much game where I come from down in the valley. I tell you again, I am Tao the artist. Word has spread among the clans that you are in need of a cave painter, so I come to paint and to bring good luck with your hunting."

The man looked around at the other hunters with their spears poised at the boy's chest. Then he turned, his eyes narrowing. "Yes, we have heard of this Tao, this image maker. But how can it be you? You are only a boy."

Tao threw back his shoulders. "I am fourteen summers, and I was taught by Graybeard himself. Two summers past I came here to get the old shaman and take him to my people. He died while down in the valley. Even then I was to come back and paint in your Secret Cavern. But your hunters were fighting with the Lake People and would let no one in."

The big man grunted and nodded in understanding.

"I was here two summers past, yet I do not know you."
He glanced around at the others. "Who among us remembers this boy?"

The hunters all shook their heads.

"Your leader, Rutar," said Tao, "he will know me."

"I am Wodak, the new leader," said the big man.
"Rutar was killed last summer by a rhino."

Tao tried to think of others who were there, but could
not. "I was here less than a day," he said. "Graybeard
and Rutar are the only ones I knew."

Wodak scowled. "So if no one knows you, how can we
be sure?"

Tao stood biting his lip, wondering how he could
make these suspicious people believe him.

Just then an old woman hobbled down the path. A
torn bison robe covered her shoulders. A faded reindeer
pelt was tied about her waist. Her legs were bowed, and
she shuffled toward the men with feet wrapped in a pair
of straw sandals. When she saw Tao she smiled broadly,
showing a row of teeth yellowed from chewing spruce
gum.

Wodak frowned. "You know this boy?"

The woman pushed the strings of gray hair out of her
eyes and hugged the bison robe tighter around her
shoulders against the morning chill. "He is the cave
painter from the Valley People," she said. "Deha remembers him from two summers ago, when he came
for Graybeard."

"You are sure of that?"

The old woman stopped to catch her breath. "Yes, he is Tao the artist. We saw him from the cave entrance as he came up the hill through the trees. I told Deha what he looked like, how he walked with a limp. She said it was him."

Wodak leaned down close to the old woman's face. Doubt still lingered in his voice. "And how would the blind one know all this?"

"It was before she lost her eyes," said the woman. "She remembers the wolf dog and how the boy walks, using his spear."

The big leader stood for a moment as if uncertain. Then he sighed and threw up his hands. "We look for a man and we find a boy."

One of the hunters spoke up. "If it is so, then let him come to the Secret Cavern. We will know soon enough if he can paint."

"All right," said Wodak, waving his hand toward the camp. "Let us find out." He turned and led the way down the path.

Tao held Ram on a short leash as he followed the men down through the tall forest of pines and hemlocks.

The old woman hobbled along behind Tao. She talked almost without stop. "I am Jema," she said. "I help feed the children, the ones in the little cave and sometimes the ones in camp. I saw many grow up, some to become

hunters, others to die before they were fifteen summers, many from sickness or the claws of wild beasts.
We miss Graybeard. It is different now that he is gone.
Now we have no healer. The knowledge of the herbs and
roots went with him."

Tao turned and smiled back at her, glad that she had
come along when she did. She reminded him of Kala,
his foster mother, the medicine woman of his clan.

"I know much of the past," Jema went on, "when the
clan was small and the roe deer many." She breathed
heavily as she hobbled down the trail. She put her
hands on her hips, took a deep breath, and said, "I knew
your mother when she was only a girl."

They had fallen some distance behind the others and
could talk freely. Tao's eyes grew wide. "You knew
Vedra?"

"Yes," said the old woman, "we played together when
we were children. She was stolen from the clan by your
father when she was only fifteen summers. That is
one of the reasons there is much anger between the
clans."

Tao nodded. "That and the raiding of the herds," he
said. He could smell the savory odor of boar and turtle
meat roasting on the cook fires as they came close to
the camp. He stopped before they entered and turned
to Jema. "Who is this Deha," he asked, "the one who remembers me?"

Jema put her finger up to her lips. "Not now," she said. "Later I will tell you."

They made their way into the camp, where a scattered collection of skin huts was set up just below the high wall of mountain.

Here, groups of women worked around the cook fires, roasting meats. Fat dripped from the long ironwood spits, sizzling and fizzing as it splashed onto the burning embers. Older men and women sat cross-legged on the ground under giant oak trees, shaving down fresh hides with sharp flint scrapers.

Naked children ran between the trees and around the huts, giggling. They threw pinecones and acorns and chased one another with willow switches.

Tao could make out a dark hole in the side of the mountain, high above the little camp. A great fire burned near the opening, and he was sure it was the entrance to the clan's Secret Cavern. Here, as with every clan, the elders and the young hunters, or Chosen Ones, would hold their rituals and ceremonies. Here the walls of the caves were painted with images of bison, horses, lions, mammoths, and other beasts, sacred offerings to the spirits of the animals.

Tired and hungry from his long journey, Tao sat in the shade under the hemlock trees and watched the women working around the cook fires.

Before going to his hut Wodak turned to Tao. "You

rest here now," he said. "Tonight the rituals will begin and you will paint."

Around noon, Jema came up with a stone bowl full of turtle meat and some earth apples. She brought along the leg bone of a deer, with strips of raw meat still attached, and dropped it in front of Ram. The wolf dog pounced on it, tearing off the meat, bolting it down in great juicy chunks. Then he lay on the ground, holding the bone between his paws, crushing it with his strong teeth.

Jema stood by and watched. "It is good to have a wolf dog," she said. "Now you hunt together like the lions."

Tao nodded toward the grasslands. "I saw the one we call Sandar last night, hunting the horses."

"You saw horses?" asked Jema.

"Yes, a small band with a stallion. The first in two summers."

Jema smiled. "Then soon others will follow. Tonight the hunters will celebrate."

There was silence for a moment. Then Tao asked again, "Tell me, who is Deha?"

Jema looked around, staring through the trees as if searching the shadows, a touch of fear in her dark eyes. "She is the blind one who lives in the cave with the Evil Children, the three orphans. She remembers you from the time you were here two summers ago."

"She lives in the cave?" said Tao. "Why?"

"Because the wild man Zugor says she is possessed

of evil spirits and must live away from the clan. Without eyes to see, she cannot escape. Yet even in her darkness she has learned to do many things. She makes music and she—" The woman fell silent as a group of children ran up to see the wolf dog.

Jema pushed them back. "The wolf eats," she said firmly. "Now let him be."

The children moved away a short distance and stood quietly, watching, their dark eyes aglow with interest.

Jema turned to Tao and lowered her voice. "Here, tonight," she whispered, "after the rituals, I will tell you more."

3

After Jema left, Tao finished his meal, enjoying the taste of the warm meat and the tangy earth apples. Then he tied the end of the leash around his wrist, stretched out on the soft hemlock needles, and fell asleep with Ram by his side.

How long he slept, he did not know, but he was awakened by a tug on the leash and the sound of Ram's deep-throated growl. He looked up quickly to see Jema standing over him. She grinned in the gathering darkness and pointed up toward the big cave. "The elders and the Chosen Ones wait in the Secret Cavern," she whispered. "It is time for the painting."

Tao rubbed his eyes and stood up. He gave the end of the leash to Jema. "Will you keep him with you till I return?" he asked.

Jema sat down beside the wolf dog. She put her arm around his warm furry shoulders and looked up at Tao.

"Go," she said. "Paint well. We will be here when you get back."

Without waiting, Tao climbed the steep path leading to the cave. A great fire burned at the entrance, casting shimmering yellow ghosts that danced across the gray walls.

A young hunter picked an evergreen torch out of the fire and led Tao through the entrance and down a long corridor. Tao was sure he was little more than a boy, perhaps twelve summers. "You are already a Chosen One?" he asked.

The boy smiled and shook his head. "Not yet," he said, "but tonight I will join the circle of new hunters, soon to become a Chosen One." His smile broadened. "And tonight I have the honor of holding the brushes and colors for your painting."

Tao felt a quick sense of pride at the boy's words. Yet he knew he would have to paint well to please these watchful elders and the hunters.

He followed the boy deep into the cave, around narrow bends and low places where they had to stoop over to keep from bumping their heads against the ceiling. The flickering torchlight cast ghostly shadows that hovered around them as they hunched along.

The air was cool and damp, and Tao heard the *drip, drip, drip* of water as it fell from the ceiling or ran down the walls, where it drained off through little cracks and crannies in the limestone floor.

They frequently squirmed on hands and knees, squeezing their way through narrow crawl spaces and under low overhangs.

Finally, Tao heard the faint sound of chanting and the clapping of sticks from deep inside the cave. *"Ho ba ho shun ga, shun ga shew, shun ga shew."* He recognized many of the words as the brave song of the hunters asking the spirits of the beasts to grant them success in the coming chase.

The singing grew louder, and around the next bend they came into a huge cavern, where the elders sat cross-legged on the stone floor. A score of young hunters danced and strutted barefoot in a wide circle, holding flaming torches high above their heads. A thick haze of white smoke filled the cavern. The stagnant air smelled strongly of burning fat and pinewood.

Blood-red images of bison, fat and ponderous, decorated the spacious cavern. Giant oxen, roe deer, mammoths, and wooly rhinos, all painted in greens, yellows, oranges, and flaming reds, trudged across the walls in a long procession, in many places making their way up across the ceiling. Some were drawn over older sketches of bears, horses, and lions.

Tao gazed at it all with open mouth as a rush of excitement raced through his veins. He took in the majestic scene, glancing around the big cavern from one end to the other. He stopped suddenly as he recognized a giant deer painted by Graybeard. He could tell the old shaman's style, the bold outline, his shading of color, the master stroke of his hand.

It felt good to be here, to paint images beside the work of all the other fine artists of the past who had left their marks on these walls for a thousand summers or more before him. This feeling of awe in the Secret Caverns followed Tao whenever he went from clan to clan, in the lakelands, in the great caverns along the riverbanks, in the Valley caves, and now here in the Mountain country.

Now before him, on the floor, lay long rows of bowl-shaped stones filled with paints—black, gray, red, yellow, and white, all made of finely ground earth mixed with clay, water, and fish oil. With these simple colors he would create his images.

Wodak stood up. He threw his mouflon robe over his shoulder and nodded, a sign that the painting was to begin. The hunters stopped dancing. They moved back, out of the way, and held their flaming torches above their heads to light up the higher reaches of the cave.

A rickety birch-wood scaffolding stood near one side of the cavern, reaching up to a blank space of wall and ceiling. Tao worked his way up the shaky structure from rung to rung and balanced himself on top. The young-boy hunter climbed up beside him with a glowing lamp of boar fat. He twined his legs around the scaffolding for support and tied the lamp securely to a crossbar with a leather thong. Then he leaned down as one of the other hunters handed him a crude wooden pallet of paints and chalks.

Tao looked at the empty wall and decided to create something different. Sandar. He would paint Sandar, since the image of the great beast was still fresh in his mind. He reached into his deerskin pouch and drew out the flat stone with the etching of the big lion he had made only a summer before. He held it up in front of him, ready to copy it line for line.

His hand shook with anticipation as he picked out a stick of charcoal from the pallet. He ran his fingers over the rough limestone wall, feeling the texture, searching for the bulges and indentations that would give his painting a feeling of depth.

With wide sweeping strokes Tao outlined the shape of the big lion. He started with the head, then the strong muscular shoulders, and the rump, with the legs tucked up under it, ready to spring. He drew Sandar climbing, creeping up toward the ceiling as if stalking his prey. He made the drawing almost as large as life, so that it covered a good part of the wall.

As he sketched in the details of the eyes, the nostrils, and the black-tipped ears, he heard a murmur of approval from the elders, and he knew that the drawing had been accepted. Now their suspicion was relieved. They knew what he could do.

In the center of the cavern, the hunters got up and

began dancing again, chanting, *"Ho ba shun ga, ho ba shun ga shew."*

The young hunter, clinging to the scaffold just below Tao, held up the pallet of colors. Tao picked out a light ocher paint, and using a boar's-tail brush, he mixed it with a zinc paste to make a tawny yellow. With broad strokes he brushed it over the outline, following the long flowing curves of the body. Then he dipped a bit of damp moss in some charred-bone powder and brushed in the dark shadows between the shoulder blades and along the ridge of the back.

The dancing and chanting stopped as Tao added the highlights. Using the zinc paste once again, he dabbed touches of white around the lips and face, over the tops of the shoulder muscles, and around the haunches. Slowly the great beast Sandar came to life.

With the painting finished, Tao looked down at the spectators. The hunters stared up in awe, their mouths open wide. The elders nodded and smiled.

Wodak paced back and forth. He kept looking up at the painting, a wide grin on his bearded face, his bare arms folded across his chest.

Tao started to climb down the scaffold.

"Wait," Wodak shouted.

Tao stopped and glanced down.

"Sandar hunts?" asked Wodak.

"Yes," said Tao, puzzled.

Wodak waved his big hand over his head, indicating the empty space on the ceiling. "Then show us what Sandar hunts," he said, "so we may hunt like the lions."

Tao felt another rush of pride. They wanted more. He tried to think of something easy, something he had done many times before.

Quickly he picked out a charcoal and outlined a bison. He drew it as if it were fleeing from the lion. He reached high up on the ceiling, working in a cramped position as he painted in the burnished colors of the humped body, the dark underbelly, and finished with the glistening white horns of a male bison.

Then with deft strokes of his charcoal, he added a row of curved lines trailing off behind it, creating the impression of an entire herd.

When Tao was finished, the hunters stared up at the bison, nodding their heads in approval.

Wodak smiled at Tao. "Your paintings live," he said. "They are real and true. Because of this the hunting will be good."

Tao felt the warmth of acceptance. He had proven himself to these distrustful people. Once again he started to climb down the scaffold.

Then from below came the words "More, more."

Tao stopped and rubbed his eyes with the back of his hand. His arms were tired, his legs stiff from working in the cramped position. He wanted to stop and rest.

But the hunters were excited now. "More, more," they shouted.

"A horse," one yelled.

Others joined in. "Yes, the horses are back. Let us see a horse."

Tao sighed, a deep weary sigh. He was pleased with his success but tired from the heat and fumes of the burning torches. Worse than that, he found the horse the most difficult drawing of all to do. The long galloping legs, the arched neck, and stately head took great pains to master.

Wodak looked up again, eyeing the still-untouched part of the ceiling. "There is still room," he said. "Let Sandar be chasing a horse."

Once again Tao climbed back up the scaffold and studied the portion of empty ceiling. The young hunter handed up a stick of charcoal, and Tao saw the pride and admiration shining in his eyes. It gave him inspiration and hope. He reached up over his head to begin his drawing. He had never even made a sketch stone or done a wall painting of a horse before. But the time had come, and now he must try.

4

A stillness fell over the big cavern. Shadows skipped across the walls and ceiling. From high on the scaffold, Tao looked down at the upturned faces watching him intently, all waiting patiently for some special magic.

He took a deep breath, then, holding on to the scaffold with one hand, he leaned back and faced the ceiling only an arm's length away. With the stick of charcoal in his free hand, he reached up and made the first wavering lines.

Starting with the head, he worked slowly, sketching freely in wide sweeps to make the painting curve up over the ceiling. Then he shaped out the arched back, drawing bold dark lines to outline the rump and flanks.

He stopped for a moment to study it. The jaw and muzzle came out all right, but the ears were too far forward for a running animal, and the neck seemed too long. He knew he should start over to get it right. But that would look as if he didn't know what he was doing. So to hide his uncertainty he decided to keep on going and make the changes as he went along.

With a trembling hand he sketched in the legs to show the animal galloping in full flight. The charcoal lines stood out sharp and bold against the gray limestone. Still something was wrong. The back legs did not look right. They looked like the branches of a dead oak tree, out of shape and bent in all the wrong places.

Tao felt the eyes staring up at him, watching his every move, waiting, questioning. To give himself time to think, he ran his finger lightly over the drawing as if measuring the distance.

Heat rose up from the flickering torches. Thick white fumes from the flaming fat burned his eyes. Sweat trickled down his cheeks and along the back of his neck.

His charcoal broke. The boy holding the pallet grinned and handed him another.

Tao smiled back at him, certain that the young boy sensed his discomfort.

Tao gritted his teeth and shook his head. Here he was, a cave painter, trained by Graybeard himself, and he could not even outline a horse, one of the most common animals shown on the walls of the Secret Caverns.

A low grumbling of voices came up from below. The hunters watched and grew restless. Tao could wait no longer. He lifted his hand to continue, when suddenly he remembered the beautiful engraving he had found on the path below the little cave. He reached into his skin pouch and took it out. His heart beat fast as he looked at it under the flickering torchlight. The lines showed up clear and sharp, the very thing he needed.

Without waiting, he began to work again. He wrapped both legs around the birch-wood scaffolding, balancing himself, leaving his hands free. Holding the engraving in one hand and the charcoal in the other, he sketched in dark bold lines, right over his first drawing. His hand followed the flowing lines of the engraving as if guided by magic.

With wild daring strokes he outlined the head, then the muscular shoulders, the strong back and flanks. The legs and hooves, which he had had so much trouble with, came alive in a beautiful, graceful gallop.

His tiredness vanished, and a wild sense of elation filled him. This, he felt sure, was the best painting he had ever done.

He left the legs on the far side of the drawing slightly detached to give a feeling of depth, an old trick Graybeard had taught him.

Then he leaned back to inspect his work. The flaming torches cast a rippling glow over the stone ceiling, creating a warm aura of light around the drawing. He was pleased. At the same time he heard the mumbling praise of the elders, and he became aware of the intense interest below. The young hunters, the leaders, and the elders gathered around, staring up at the drawing, as if in a trance.

At the same time, he felt a tinge of guilt. He did not want to deceive them, for the drawing they so admired was not entirely his, but a copy of the beautiful engraving he held in his hand. He must find a way to tell them after the rituals were over.

He put down his charcoal. Then he mixed a deep red mud with a dab of yellow clay from the pallet the young hunter was holding, blending it together until it became a bright reddish brown. With a sponge made from a swab of bison hide, he brushed this over the entire body, painting it heavily on the back and shoulders. A bit of charcoal powder stirred in fish oil and painted on the inside of the legs and under the neck and belly filled in the shadows. Next he dabbed on spots of white-chalk water to create highlights around the head and shoulders.

Slowly the painting came alive, a roan stallion fleeing across the plains, with Sandar crouching close beside it, ready to spring.

Tao worked steadily, putting in the finishing touches. Finally the painting was done. Tao gazed up at it with pride, his face and chest covered with sweat from the tension and from the heat of the flaming torches.

Once more the chanting and dancing began, and now other young men took their turns at the wall. A few worked below, doing crude stick pictures of deer and ibex. One climbed up the rickety scaffolding as it rocked and swayed under his weight. He painted an ill-shaped image of a red-and-black bull. Another clambered up and drew a stilted figure of what was meant to be a bear. Some of the young hunters simply pressed their palms against the wall, and taking a mouthful of chalk water, spewed it out between their outspread fingers, leaving an imprint of their hands.

All were clumsy and untrained, for, since Graybeard's death, none had been taught even the simplest lessons of art or painting.

It was late, but now the ceremonies would begin and go on and on into the early morning.

Exhausted, his work done, Tao climbed down from the scaffold. He took one of the flaming torches and made his way out of the cavern, crawling back through the narrow winding tunnels until he reached the entrance.

He found Jema back under the hemlocks, still waiting for him with Ram by her side. She stood up as Tao approached with the torch. The night was quiet, and they were alone.

"The elders were pleased?" asked Jema.

"Yes," said Tao. "It was good, and soon the hunting can begin." Carefully Tao took the engraving of the horse from his pouch. He held it up in the torchlight so Jema could see. "I must tell the elders, this drawing is not mine but belongs to another. I used it tonight in the paintings."

Jema looked at the slate stone and gasped. "No," she whispered, "say nothing."

Tao was puzzled by her words.

"It was made by Deha, who lives in the cave with the orphans, the Evil Children," said Jema.

"The blind one?"

"Yes," said Jema. "You see, Deha fell from a tree while collecting honey two summers ago. Her eyes went dark. She has seen nothing since."

Tao studied the engraving once again under the torch-light. The lines flowed over the slate stone without a flaw, so fine, so skillfully etched. "She is blind," he said, "yet she can do this?"

"Her eyes remember the things she once saw," said Jema. "Her fingers feel the grooves of the tracings on the stone and tell her how to make the lines." The woman stopped for a moment and looked around. "But tell no one," she said. "If Deha is caught making images, she could be banished from the clan and sent up into the mountains. Without eyes she would soon starve or be killed by the hyenas. Graybeard told us how you started to draw when you were only a child and were punished for it. So you know the taboos better than any of us."

Tao knew what Jema meant. He remembered how he too had lived with the cruel taboos, evicted from the clan for drawing in the sand, living as an outcast until Graybeard found him. Now he wondered about this remarkable girl who could make such beautiful images. "But why must she live in a cave?"

Jema looked around again, searching the trees and bushes, peering into the darkness. She hesitated for a moment, then whispered, "It is because of Zugor, the mad shaman," she whispered. "When Graybeard died, Zugor came out of the forest and sought to take the old man's place. With curses and spells he holds the clan in his power. Because Deha is blind, Zugor claims she is possessed of demons. He has tried to cure her with his wild magic but cannot, so he keeps her in the little cave to protect the clan people from her evil spirits."

Tao winced. "Wodak and the elders believe this?"

Jema put her finger to her lips. "Speak low," she said, glancing around again. "Zugor is like a ghost. He is everywhere, spying, listening. If the people go against his wishes, he puts a curse on them.

"Not long ago, Rutar was our leader. He did not fear the mad shaman, and chased him out of the clan. Zugor put a curse on him. Rutar only laughed. But the next day, while hunting, he was killed by the rhino.

"The elders called it an omen. Now they fear Zugor and do his bidding. If not, Zugor threatens to stop the rains and bring starvation. The hunters hate him for this but fear his curses."

"And the children," Tao asked, "why are they evil?"

"Their heads are swollen," said Jema. "Their arms and legs are crooked like the branches of a dead tree."

"They are sick?" said Tao.

Jema hesitated and shrugged. "If so, I don't know. Maybe Zugor is right. He says they too are possessed by the evil spirits and must be kept away from the clan."

Tao groaned and shook his head sadly. "Because he sees no reason for the sickness, he calls it evil. My foster mother, Kala, is an herb woman. She will have medicine for this." Tao was silent for a moment. Then he said, "If I could go to this blind girl and these children, I could tell Kala what I see. Maybe she will know what to do."

Jema shook her head. "I bring them leftovers from the cook fires every day, but I cannot take you with me. It would be too dangerous. Zugor would put a curse on me." She looked around in the darkness, her eyes filled with fear. "No, you cannot go with me, but you can watch where I go."

Tao caught her meaning and smiled.

"You are not afraid?" she asked.

The boy shook his head. "I have heard too many empty threats, I have broken too many senseless taboos. No, I am not afraid."

As she turned to go, Jema looked back and whispered, "Tomorrow morning, then."

5

Early the next morning, Tao watched Jema walk out of camp and trudge up the path through the hemlock trees. She stooped over, carrying a skin sack of dried food in one hand, and a water bag made of bison gut slung over her shoulder.

Tao let her get far ahead until she was almost out of sight. Then he put Ram on the leash and followed. The sun had just come up, sending golden shafts of light through the trees. The morning air smelled fresh and damp. High overhead a big black woodpecker drummed on a dead spruce, its *rat-tat-tat* ringing throughout the forest. Bright red crossbills chirped and twittered as they hopped from branch to branch, probing for seeds in the hemlock cones.

When he came to the foot of the mountain, Tao saw Jema disappear into the dark opening of the little cave. He waited awhile, then started up the narrow ledge. The entrance to the cave was partially hidden by a group of stunted pine trees. Halfway there he heard the melodic notes of the flute once again, rising and falling on the morning air.

Tao listened for a moment. Then he went on, climbing slowly. He had almost reached the opening when the music stopped. Quietly he stepped over the threshold and looked around. His eyes became adjusted to the dim light, and he saw the small fire burning low on the hearth in the center of the cave. A large flat stone sat on the floor beside it, and Tao could tell it was used as a table for cracking nuts or cutting tubers. Four sleeping mats of dry grass lay in a row along one side of the cave. Sunlight streamed through the entrance, blending into the darkness toward the back of the cave.

Jema turned toward him. She smiled but said nothing, and went back to her work.

Tao saw three children come out of the shadows. They could barely walk, hobbling into the light on spindly legs, gathering around Jema as she tipped up the water bag and gave each a drink. She opened the sack of cooked tubers and spread them out on the flat stone. The children reached for them hungrily, stuffing them into their mouths.

Stooped and work-worn, Jema took care of the sick children with gentle patience, making sure each one got a share of the simple foods. Tao watched her, and again she reminded him of his foster mother, Kala, a woman who cared for others, thinking little of her own needs and wishes.

Then Tao glanced around the little room, peering into the shadows, looking for the girl, Deha. But she was not to be seen. He was about to ask Jema, when the children came toward him. Hardly able to stand, they stared up at him through sunken eyes, their swollen heads bobbing on thin, frail bodies. Legs and arms wobbled like knobby sticks. Tattered shreds of deerskin served as clothing. Hanks of green straw, tied around their feet, made do for sandals.

Tao tried to guess their ages, maybe four or five summers, he thought. He stepped farther into the cave. At that moment the children saw Ram. They stopped eating and hobbled over to the wolf dog, their eyes wide now as they mumbled with excitement, "Hoo, hoo, look, look." Ram sniffed at them and wagged his tail. They reached out and ruffled his furry back and shoulders. Tao let him off the leash, and the children sat on the floor, giggling and squealing as he walked around them, licking their faces, playing with them.

It was then the girl came out. She walked in quietly from the shadows in the back of the cave. She too was thin. But she stood tall and graceful, an old antelope skin draped over one shoulder. Tao knew it was Deha. She came into the light and he saw her eyes, not white or cloudy like other blind people he had seen, but shiny black against her pale face. Except for her blank stare it was hard to tell she could not see.

Ram saw her too. He left the children and ran over to her. He cocked his head to one side and looked up at her, then licked her hand and whimpered softly.

Deha smiled. She knelt down beside him and scratched his head, speaking to him quietly. Ram loved the attention. Deha stood up, and Ram moved close to her and pressed against her legs, as if he knew she needed protection.

Then Deha turned in Tao's direction, sensing he was there. Yet she did not come forward. Instead she stayed in the background, still partially hidden in the shadows, quiet and shy.

Jema came over and stood beside the boy. "It is Tao of the Valley People," she said.

Deha nodded. She folded her hands in front of her and bowed slightly. "Welcome, Tao. We saw you yesterday, coming up the hill with your wolf dog."

"You saw?" asked Tao, puzzled.

The girl shook her head. "I mean the children did. They are my eyes. They spend long hours looking down through the trees. There is little they do not see."

Jema put her hand on the boy's arm. "Last night Tao painted for the hunting ceremony in the big cave," she said proudly. "Wodak and the elders are pleased. They say Tao's paintings are true and real."

Deha smiled and her voice rose with interest. "Ah, you

painted in the Secret Cavern. Quick, tell me, what image did you make?"

"I drew Sandar the cave lion," said Tao, "and a bison."

Deha smiled. "If only I could see them," she said sadly.

Tao reached into his skin pouch and took out the engraving. "Also I found your beautiful sketch stone and used it as a guide to paint a galloping horse."

Deha drew in her breath and put her hands up to her mouth. "It must be the one I dropped some days ago."

Tao hastened to explain. "It was on the path just below the cave," he said. "Ram found it as we passed."

A look of fear flashed in her eyes.

Jema quickly assured her. "Don't be afraid," she said. "He told no one."

Tao held out the sketch stone. "It is beautiful," he said, "the most perfect sketch I have ever seen. Now I must return it."

The girl pulled back. "No, no," she said quietly. "It is yours to keep. Use it whenever you wish. It will be good to know that my drawing is painted on the walls of many Secret Caverns."

"It is so well done," Tao said. "The lines are sharply drawn and easy to follow. How did you learn such art?"

"Just as you did," said Deha. "I had the best teacher."

Startled, Tao could think of only one name. "Graybeard?"

Deha nodded. "When I was a little girl I used to

scratch drawings of birds and flowers in the sand with a pointed stick. One day Graybeard saw me. Quickly I tried to rub it out, but he stopped me. Then he sat me down and showed me how to scratch images of bears and mammoths on pieces of slate. I could still see then, and even though he knew I could never be a Chosen One, he taught me in secret whenever he came to our clan. Not long before he died, he told me about you, how good you were and how you would one day be a cave painter for all the clans."

Tao smiled but quickly added, "I will try, but I know none will ever be as good as Graybeard."

"Oh, but you will," said Deha. "That is why you must teach others, so that his art may live."

Tao smiled, wishing it were that easy. "Your drawing shows much strength and skill," he said. "Have you done others?"

Jema spoke up. "Deha sketches often when she is not playing the flute or taking care of the children." She turned toward the girl. "Show Tao your slates. He will keep your secret."

Deha went far back into the cave and returned a moment later with a handful of slates. "I keep only the best ones," she said, holding them out to Tao. "I hide them well, for I must be careful."

Tao took them out close to the entrance, where there was more light. One by one he studied them, a bison, a mammoth, a rhino, a reindeer, and a cave lion. They showed the same bold style she had used with the galloping horse.

"You saw the lion?" Tao asked.

"Yes, the big one, Sandar. I saw him three summers ago, when I still had my eyes. Now I can draw him from memory."

"Then you can also teach and make slates so others can use them as guides to paint in the Secret Caverns," Tao said.

Deha shook her head. "For me the world is dark. I cannot teach what I cannot see." She shrugged. "Besides, it is taboo for a woman to make images."

Tao stood there admiring the slates, turning them over in his hands. She can do all this, he thought, yet it is taboo. Why must it be like this? Why could she not teach with her hands and with the touch of her fingers? Why could she not carve and make engravings and ornaments from things of the earth, if only they would let her?

"In our clan," he said, "it is not taboo for a woman to make things of beauty from flowers and leaves. She cannot go into the Secret Cavern, but she may draw on stones or make carvings of wood and ivory."

Eager to hear more, Deha stepped closer, away from the shadows.

Tao looked at her and gasped. Long red welts ran down her arms and legs. One crossed her face from her left ear across the bridge of her nose to her cheek. Tao groaned and turned to Jema. "She has been beaten?" he said.

Jema nodded. "Yes, each time the moon is full, Zugor beats her with a willow switch to drive out the demons. It is his magic to make her see again." Jema threw up her hands and sighed. "But it is no good, she still lives in the dark."

Tao shook his head in disbelief. "Wodak and the elders allow this?"

Jema walked to the entrance and glanced around outside. Then she came back and whispered, "As I told you, Zugor holds the clan in his power with curses, spells, and demons. All the people say his mother was a Neander, a woman of the hairy people of a time long ago."

Tao frowned. "A Neander, here in the clan?"

"Yes," said Jema, "and he works vile magic. I have seen the sun go dark and fire come down from the sky and light the grasslands as Zugor watched and shook his grisly rattle. One time I felt the earth shake while the hairy one danced around like a madman."

Tao shook his head. He remembered last summer when he was drawing in a cave and the earth shook. His paints spilled, and rocks tumbled from the ceiling. Everyone felt it, everyone spoke of it. He threw back his head and laughed. "And they think Zugor did this all by himself?"

"Yes, it is so," said Jema. "It was the same day we saw

Rutar carried home dead, killed by Tonda the rhino after Zugor put a curse on him. It is he who casts the spells and calls up the spirits."

Tao shrugged. He looked at Deha and wondered about her eyes, thinking maybe she might be healed someday by medicines and potions. Then almost without meaning to he blurted out, "I know one who can cure you."

A wisp of a smile crossed Deha's face, a smile of doubt, as if she had heard such promises before. "I am listening," she said.

"She is Kala of the Valley People."

"Yes, I have heard of her," said Deha. "Is she not a sorcerer?"

"No, no, never," said Tao, shaking his head. "She uses no spells or witchery."

Deha's face brightened. "You mean she cures by herbs and potions and things of the earth that heal, not by magic?"

"Yes," said Tao, "she uses all the plants, all the oils and remedies she learned from Graybeard."

Deha took a step closer. She looked at Tao as if she could see him, and spoke softly, almost under her breath. "If this is possible," she said quietly, "if she could really do this, I would like to go to her."

"Then I will take you," said Tao.

She stood there for a moment, her hand on Ram's shoulder, her fingers curling and twining in his soft fur.

Slowly her face fell and she shrugged. "But I am sure the elders will not allow it."

"But why?"

"Because Zugor will call up the demons and make trouble. He will cast his spells and frighten the elders." She turned as if she were looking at the children. "They will say we are all possessed of the evil spirits, and here we must stay."

Jema broke in, forgetting her fears for the moment. "But if Tao can take you to the Land of the Valley People, you will be free of Zugor."

"Jema is right," said Tao. "Tomorrow morning I will speak with Wodak and the elders before Zugor has a chance to frighten them with his wild threats. If they give their permission, we will go down across the valley and be gone before Zugor has a chance to call up his demons."

"But what about the children?" said Deha.

"I will stay with the children," said Jema. "You go with Tao to the medicine woman. Come back with new eyes. The children will be waiting for you."

There was a short silence. Deha put her hands up to her cheeks and shook her head. "It is too good," she said. "It is too much to hope for."

"It can happen," said Tao. Then to cheer things up, he added, "And tonight we will have a feast."

Jema chuckled. "On what, on dry tubers and ground beans?"

"No," said Tao. "On duck eggs and mushrooms, on chestnuts and mussels, or whatever else I can find."

The children caught the excitement. They chattered excitedly as they looked forward to the coming treat.

Tao was about to leave, when he heard Ram growl. The pine shrubs rustled just outside the entrance.

Tao went out and looked around. He came back shaking his head. "It's gone," he said. "Maybe it was an ibex or a young bear."

Jema's face grew white with fear. "It was Zugor," she whispered, "I know it. He lives in a dingy cave up in the mountains but comes down to spy on the people."

"Do you think he heard?" asked Deha.

Jema shook her head. "We spoke low, but his ears are sharp."

"Let Ram stay here," said Tao. "Even Zugor will not bother you as long as the wolf dog is here." He smiled to reassure them, then he picked up his spear and started down toward the river.

6

With his skin pouch slung over his shoulder, Tao made his way along the overgrown path and into the dark hemlock forest. Here and there, shafts of afternoon sunlight filtered through the canopy of branches. He followed the trail down to where the river made its narrow turn toward the Great Waters. Here, along the water's edge, he could scoop up mussels or catch frogs or carp or maybe some crawfish.

He stood on the bank and watched the clear water ripple over the white gravel and around the moss-covered boulders. Clumps of blue flags and pink mallows grew along the shoreline, where swarms of fat bumblebees, yellow with pollen, droned from flower to flower.

Across the shallows he spotted two turtles sunning themselves on a half-sunken log. One was large, the other about the size of a clamshell. Together they would make a tasty stew for the children. Tao crept up quietly behind a clump of reeds. If he could get close enough, he might be able to grab them before they scrambled into the water.

He walked slowly, one step at a time, so as not to splash. As he came closer he parted the reeds and peered through. The turtles sat with their heads up, their green-striped throats pulsating as the afternoon sun glinted off their shiny wet backs.

Quietly, Tao pushed his spear into the sand to keep it from floating away. Then he turned and made ready to pounce. One more step and he would be close enough to grasp them, one in each hand.

The shallow water swirled around his legs. He leaned over slowly, balancing himself. Just then a stone slipped under his bad foot. He started to fall. The turtles caught the movement. Their eyes blinked, their heads went down, and they plunged into the water.

As he toppled forward, Tao reached out and managed to catch the smaller one, grabbing it by the back of the shell. It struggled to get free, its strong claws scratching against his fingers. He held on tightly and fell headfirst into the river. He came up spitting water, with the little turtle in his hand. He sat there for a moment, with the water swirling around him. At first he felt foolish. Then he grinned. He looked down at himself, squatting up to his hips in water, and he looked at the little turtle, still clawing at the air but going nowhere. He threw back his head and laughed till the tears ran down his cheeks. Then he leaned down, opened his hand, and let the little turtle go. With a flurry of kicks it swam away and disappeared into the weeds.

Tao got to his feet and picked up his spear. He still needed something for the feast he had promised the children; a rabbit, a squirrel, or a goose. But the afternoon was getting late and there was not much time.

He waded back across the shallows. There he made his way along the bank, searching through the reeds, waiting for a duck to fly up. Then, if he were lucky, he might find the nest and bring back a few eggs.

After a long search he found nothing. He could not go back without some offering of food, no matter how small, so he decided to gather hazelnuts and handfuls of the big oyster mushrooms he had seen on his way down the mountain.

He turned to leave, when out of the corner of his eye he noticed a glint of silver out on the water. He watched the spot closely for a moment and saw it flash again. His heart beat fast. He hoped it was not just the afternoon sun reflecting on the ripples. He stood there watching, and a moment later, he saw it again.

This time he did not wait. He plunged into the shallows, heading for the spot. Then he saw it up close, a big spring salmon fighting its way upstream to the breeding grounds. Its silvery pink body shimmered in the sunlight as it swam over the white gravel. He reached down and grabbed it by the tail. But it was strong and slippery. It wriggled out of his grasp and headed for deeper water.

Tao chased after it, stumbling, splashing through the water. With the flat of his spear he pushed it toward shore. Twice more it got away and escaped into the ripples, but little by little he drove it close to the bank. Finally he caught it and flipped it up into the weeds, where it lay splashing and flapping about. He grabbed it by the tail and dragged it up onshore. It was a big fish, longer than his arm and heavy with eggs.

He took a leather thong from his deerskin pouch, passed it through the mouth and gills, and slung the fish over his shoulder. He leaned forward as he trudged up the hill, the better to balance the weight of the big fish on his back.

On his way up through the woods, he stopped and pried off clumps of oyster mushrooms from a rotting hickory stump. These he stuffed into his skin pouch, an extra treat for the feast.

He picked up his spear and waited a moment to catch his breath before climbing higher. He turned and looked back toward the river, and over the tops of the hemlocks he could see the sparkling waters far below. A big orange sun hung low, touching the tops of the distant hills. A long string of white swans flew across the horizon, silhouetted against the pink sky. He watched for a while, caught up in the beauty of the scene, unable to turn away.

He looked down again to where the river narrowed in its turn toward the sea. He smiled and, feeling pleased with his good luck, he shouted, "Thank you, Great Waters, for sending me a great fish, and the children of the little cave thank you for a great feast."

Then, as the sun began to dip behind the hills, Tao turned and started up the winding path. He had gone only a few steps when he saw the laurel bushes in front of him shake. He stopped, dropped his fish to the ground, and held up his spear, ready to throw.

All at once a wild howl filled the air, and a moment later a grubby little man jumped out of the shadows. He hunched over and planted himself directly in Tao's path. He wore the ragged skin of a hyena around his gaunt body. Like a hideous ornament, the dried skull of a raven lay draped over his left shoulder. His long hair hung down in matted strings all the way to his knees, and he smelled strongly of moldy wood. He was the ugliest man Tao had ever seen.

His words hissed as he spoke through missing teeth. "Go home," he sneered, "go home to your Valley People and stay out of the mountains. You are not wanted here."

From all he had heard, Tao knew it was Zugor, the ogre, the old mossback of the forest. His appearance was frightening, but Tao refused to be bullied by his silly threats. He glared back at the man. "I have reason to be here," he said. "I will leave when I am ready."

As the old man stood there leering at him, a night breeze moaned through the branches of the hemlock trees. Tao felt a chill run up the back of his neck.

"Your work is finished," Zugor snarled. "Take your wolf dog and go." He shook the jawbone of a bison in Tao's face, rattling the loose teeth. "But you go alone," he said. "The blind girl will stay here."

Tao winced. Zugor had been listening and already knew their plans. He grit his teeth and took a deep breath, more determined than ever that the snooping old man should not stop him. How often had he been taught, "Look up to your elders and learn"? But this was no elder; this was a wild man of the woods, no wiser than the animals.

Tao wrapped his bad leg around his spear, threw the big salmon over his shoulder, and advanced toward Zugor. "Get out of my way," he said. "You are no shaman. Your foolish threats frighten no one."

Zugor refused to move. Tao barged into him, but the wizened old man stood like a rock. Tao fell back, startled. Still Zugor did not lift a hand to strike him. Instead his green eyes flashed in anger. The dark spaces between his teeth made him appear doubly witless as he screamed, "I will cure the girl. I alone know how to drive out her demons."

Tao's mouth fell open, dumbfounded. "With what?" he cried. "With toad's eyes and bear claws or by thrashings with willow sticks? Is that the only healing you know?"

Zugor drew himself up and spread out his arms, trembling with rage. "It is magic," he yelled, "a magic of the spirits that you know nothing about. I alone know the spells." He held up the foot of an owl, tied to a leather thong, and dangled it in front of Tao's face. "I alone have the amulets to cure the darkness. So leave the girl here and get out of the mountains. Go back to your medicine woman and your people."

Tao cringed but tried to hide his fear. Zugor appeared frail and aged, but Tao knew he was as tough as an old hickory tree. Yet he had a sickness that was not of the body. He lived in a world of demons and spirits, so caught up in superstition and lies, he could no longer tell truth from fakery.

As Tao walked past, the old man made no further attempt to stop him. Instead he followed a short way, screaming and shouting, his shrill voice echoing in the boy's ears. "A curse on you," he yelled, "and a curse on your people. If the girl leaves here, the mountain demons will follow you. Your streams will become foul. Your fish will turn sour and rot in your mouth . . ."

Tao went on trying to ignore the wild threats. When he reached the foot of the mountain, Jema came down to meet him. She took the big fish from his shoulder, and together they climbed the rest of the way.

Deha and the children were delighted with the salmon. Jema started a fire and cut the fish into pieces, which she roasted on spits of willow reeds. The mushrooms simmered in the fish oil, sizzling on the hearthstones. For Deha and the children it was the first real treat in a long time, a welcome change from dried tubers and ground beans.

After the feast they all sat around the fire, laughing and singing. Later, when the children were fast asleep, Jema, Deha, and Tao sat up, talking about Deha's upcoming visit to the Land of the Valley People.

7

The following morning, Tao and Deha started for camp, while Jema stayed with the children. They left early, for Tao wanted to speak with Wodak and the elders before Zugor had a chance to interfere. Ram went on ahead as Tao guided Deha down along the narrow ledge.

When they reached the foot of the cliff, Tao tied the cedar-root leash to Ram's collar and gave the other end to Deha. She twined it around her right hand and held it tightly.

Ram looked up at her and pressed against her legs. Then with a low whimper he led her carefully along the dark path through the hemlock forest as though he had done it many times before.

Bright shafts of sunlight filtered through the trees, and small flocks of wood pigeons fluttered up as they passed. They soon came to the little camp, where the early morning cook fires sent up misty columns of white smoke.

Deha held Ram close and waited under a big elm tree near the edge of camp, while Tao went in to talk with Wodak.

The big leader came out of his bearskin hut, rubbing his eyes with one hand and clawing at his beard with the other. He looked at Tao and frowned. "You leave so soon?" he asked. He stopped in front of Tao and folded his arms across his chest. "I spoke with the elders last night. We thought it would be good if you stayed awhile and showed our young hunters how to draw and paint. Since Graybeard is gone, there is no one here to teach them."

Tao smiled, pleased by Wodak's words of praise. "Someday soon I will come back," he said. Then he nodded toward Deha. "But first I would like to take the blind girl home to my people. I am sure Kala, our medicine woman, can give her new sight."

Wodak scowled as he saw Deha standing under the big tree near the edge of camp. He shook his head and spoke sharply. "She must stay there," he said. "She cannot come into camp. It is taboo. If Zugor sees he will call down the demons."

Tao turned to Deha and told her to stay where she was. Then he turned back to Wodak. "But if the girl goes with me, she will be out of your keeping and you and the elders will not be to blame."

Wodak tugged at his beard as he thought for a moment. Then he glanced around cautiously. "Yes, that could be," he said. "That could be good if the elders are willing. Let us see." He turned to face the center of camp, then tilted his head back and cupped his hands around his mouth. "Gardo," he shouted, "Notar, Bemm, all the elders, come."

One by one, seven old, gray-headed men crawled out of their skin huts. They came from all over camp and gathered around Wodak. They grumbled and groaned, swinging their arms to warm themselves against the early morning chill.

Wodak waited until they were all assembled, then he spoke. "Today, Tao goes home to his Valley People. He would take the blind girl, Deha, with him. There, Kala the medicine woman will seek to drive out her demons." He looked from one to another. "What do you say?"

For the first time, the elders saw Deha standing near the edge of camp. They shook their heads and mumbled and moved back as if they might be tainted by the sight of her.

Wodak paced back and forth, waiting for an answer. Finally he asked, "Well, Gardo, what do they say?"

Gardo shuffled forward and whispered in Wodak's ear.

Wodak frowned and turned to Tao. "You are sure this magic can be done and that the girl will not return with her demons?"

"Kala has the herbs and oils," said Tao. "She will know what to do."

Again the elders milled about. They glanced at Deha, then spoke quietly amongst themselves.

Little by little, small groups of clan people drifted toward the center of camp where Tao and Wodak were standing. They gathered around the elders, listening. They looked at Deha and shook their heads. Some groaned and put their hands over their faces.

Finally Notar spoke up. "The wild man Zugor says the girl is possessed of evil demons. If Tao takes her away, we will be free of her, and her demons, too." He glanced around at the others for agreement, then turned back to Wodak. "We say, then, let her go."

Tao took a deep breath and smiled, hardly daring to believe they had agreed so easily.

The clan people continued to gather. They cast side glances at Deha, still standing patiently in the shadow of the big elm tree. They nodded and pointed and shook their heads, muttering under their breaths.

Without waiting, Tao walked over to get Deha before the elders changed their minds.

He had taken only a few steps when a high-pitched, rasping voice shouted, "Stop!"

All talk ceased. The elders stepped aside and opened a path for Zugor as the mad shaman pushed his way into the clearing, waving his hands over his head, chasing away a cloud of flies attracted by the half-cured fox pelt flung around his neck. The people moved back, afraid to get too close. They eyed him cautiously, as if he were an evil spirit or a ghost.

Tao saw the look of fear in Wodak's eyes and in the eyes of the elders.

The wild man glared at the people. He pointed a bony finger in their faces. "Go," he shrieked, "go back to your huts." He looked at Deha, then pointed in her direction. "This girl is possessed by the evil fiends of darkness. As long as demons live in her body, she must stay in the cave so that they will not poison other members of the clan."

Tao felt the heat of anger churn in the pit of his stomach. He could not stand by and listen to these sniveling lies. He had to speak up. "Do not listen to him," Tao cried. "He speaks only of doom and misery. He seeks to frighten you with curses and evil spells. But he has no power. He talks of demons, of ghosts and evil spirits. Where are they? I see none. If the girl goes with me, she may see again. If she stays here, he will beat her with willow switches and she will live in darkness for the rest of her life."

Zugor hissed and glowered at the boy. His hair hung down over his face like the hair of a brush pig. He wheezed when he spoke. "I warned you, your work here is finished. Take your wolf dog and get out." He shook a bone rattle in Tao's face. "But you go without the girl."

Tao knew he should hold his tongue, but anger made him reckless. Determined not to back down, he stepped forward and pointed his spear at the old man's chest.

The clan people gasped.

"I have the word of Wodak and the elders," said Tao. "You cannot stop me."

Zugor turned toward the crowd, waving his hands to chase away the flies still buzzing around his face. He trembled with rage to think that a mere boy would challenge him in front of the entire clan. Stuttering and spitting, he pointed at Deha again. "If that girl is allowed to go, I will put a curse on this clan."

The elders fell back, stumbling over one another, shaking their heads with fear.

Tao groaned. If Zugor continued with his threats, Wodak and the elders would go back on their word. He glanced at Deha and saw the disappointment on her face. Her one chance to escape her life of darkness was slipping away.

Zugor turned again, his long strings of dirty hair swirling around him. He glowered at the clan people and shook his bone rattle over his head. "If this girl leaves, her demons will stay here in the mountains to seek out another victim. Which one of you will be the next to go blind?"

The elders cowered. They shrank from this madman, uncertain, yet unwilling to question his powers.

Tao turned on the old man, desperately trying to think

of some way to call his bluff. "Your magic brings only death and suffering," he shouted. "You have no magic for good."

Zugor sneered at the boy. "And what kind of magic do *you* have? You say your Kala can cure this blind one. If she can do this, why did she not cure your bad foot?"

The words took Tao by surprise. He could think of nothing to say.

Zugor danced around and jumped up and down. "Tee-hee-hee," he laughed, slapping his thigh and looking at the clan people. "You see, you see, he cannot answer."

Tao's temper flared. He blurted out, "Kala lives by truth. You live by evil spells and curses. Even I can do your stupid magic."

The old man's eyes narrowed. "And what kind of wizardry can you do?"

For a moment Tao hesitated, his mind racing ahead, trying to think of something, anything. He looked beyond the clearing at the high evergreen trees, at the clumps of laurel bushes and the thick mounds of oak ferns and mosses. Then he remembered an old trick Graybeard had taught him. With a half smile he turned and threw the challenge back in Zugor's face. "I can bring life out of fire."

Baffled, Wodak and the clan people listened with wonder. In spite of their fear of demons and evil spirits, they pressed closer, their interests aroused.

"You lie," said Zugor. "Words are easy. Let us see the deed."

Tao stepped up and stared him in the eyes. "If I do this thing, will you let the girl go without putting a curse on this clan?"

Zugor scowled. "First show us the magic, then I will decide."

Tao turned to Wodak for an answer.

The big leader glanced around, uncertain.

Tao could tell that Wodak was interested. He wanted to see the game played out but could not openly say the word. "I am not sure," said the big leader. "You can go back to your people, but we must stay here and live with this man and his curses."

The clan people shook their heads, their faces, like Wodak's, filled with indecision.

Tao turned to them. "What do you say? If I can do this magic, will you let the girl go?"

The elders spoke in undertones, whispering and glancing at Zugor. They feared this wild man. But now they also wanted to see the magic. They wanted to see who would win.

Gardo shook a bony old fist over his head. "I say let Tao work his magic. If he can bring forth life from fire, he must have power over the spirits as well as Zugor. Then let him take the girl."

Now all the elders turned and looked in Tao's direction. First one, then another and another cried out, "Good. Let us see the magic."

Tao turned on Zugor. "You heard the clan people give their word. If I bring forth life from fire, will you give up the girl?"

Zugor frowned. Then he spit in the dirt. "And if you cannot do this thing, then what do you give up?"

Tao looked at him in surprise. He had not thought of that. He looked around the little camp, trying to think of what he could offer. He saw the rows of faces, the women in the background holding the babies, the children watching, their dark eyes wondering, all waiting for his answer. He held up his spear. "This I will give if I fail."

Zugor shook his head. "We have many spears."

Tao tried again. "A freshly killed bison calf."

Once more Zugor shook his head. "Our hunters can give the same," he said.

Tao shrugged. "What, then?"

Zugor turned, a sneering grin on his face. "Your wolf dog."

Tao cringed. He could not think of Ram being led about by this cruel man. He glanced around at the elders. He saw Wodak, Gardo, and the others standing there, waiting for an answer. The clan people stared at him.

Tao looked over at Deha, still holding Ram close on

the leash, and he saw the question in her eyes. Could Tao really bring forth life from fire?

Tao had seen it done before, yet it did not always work. But he had made the challenge, so now he must try.

The clan people pressed closer, all eyes on Tao.

Wodak raised his hand for silence. "Now, let the spirits tell us which one is right, Zugor or the boy."

8

The magic Tao hoped for was a whim of nature, not always to be counted on. But this place, at the foot of the mountain, with its mossy knolls and shady glens, seemed right for it.

Morning mist still rose from the damp earth as Tao gathered an armful of fallen oak branches. He selected a likely spot—a low mound of moss between a stand of juniper trees.

The elders and the clan people gathered around to watch as Tao took out his firestones. He struck some sparks onto a handful of dry tinder until smoke began to rise from the clump. Then he snatched it up and held it close to his face, blowing on it. Quickly it burst into flames. He placed it on the moss and added a handful of kindling. As the fire licked up, Tao carefully laid the dry oak wood on top.

Within a few moments, the fire burned brightly, heating up the surrounding moss.

The people pressed close, staring intently into the flames. Wodak and Gardo stood by, their arms folded across their chests, waiting to see the magic of new life.

Zugor hovered over the boy's shoulder, smirking, his sharp, green eyes sparkling in the light.

For a long while the fire crackled and burned and nothing happened. Tao poked at the blaze with a long stick as the flames consumed the remaining pieces of wood. Then he spread out the embers to warm more of the surrounding moss. He waited, holding his breath, hoping any moment to see a living thing rise up out of the flames. Desperately he blew on the fire. He fanned it with a hemlock branch to make it burn brighter. All was quiet save for the crackling of the flames. Still nothing happened. No ghost, no spirit rose from the smouldering embers.

The clan people grew restless, milling around the fire, mumbling darkly to themselves.

Zugor shook his rattle over his head. "Ah-ha," he cackled, "where is the life? What kind of magic is here? Nothing, I tell you, nothing!" He snarled with glee, shouting at the people. "Go back to your huts," he said. "The magic is over." He turned to Gardo, who was staring into the flames, waiting. "Take the girl back to the cave," he ordered.

"Wait," said Tao. "The fire still burns. It is not over yet."

Hurriedly the boy gathered more wood. With the end

of his spear he carried some embers to a spot nearby. He laid more kindling on and watched the flames come back to life. Then he threw on more dry wood. He fanned it again with the hemlock branch, and the fire flared up.

Long moments passed, and again nothing happened. The clan people grumbled. Some of them turned away and walked back to their huts.

Tao watched, biting his lip, waiting. From down in the valley he could hear the chorus of spring frogs in the ponds. He glanced over at Ram and saw the wolf dog staring at him, his head cocked to one side as if in question. Then he looked down again at the fire, but saw only the dancing yellow flames.

"Tee-hee-hee," Zugor laughed. "Now I have a wolf dog," he said, walking toward Deha.

Tao heard Ram growl. "Not yet!" he shouted. "Not just yet."

Once more he poked at the fire, spreading out the flames to cover more of the moss, feeling the sting of defeat in the pit of his stomach.

"Nothing," said Gardo, "all this for nothing. The girl will have to go back to the cave."

Tao saw the dashed hopes on Wodak's face as he continued to stare into the empty fire.

Zugor cackled again. "The wolf dog will hunt for me and ward off my demons."

Tao heard some of the elders muttering, walking

away. Desperately he poked at the embers again, spreading them out across the moss. Here and there a small flame licked up as white curls of smoke rose out of the heated moss. Tao grit his teeth to hide his disappointment.

Then he heard Wodak shout, "Look, look! Coming out of the fire, look!"

Tao turned to see the small creature he had been waiting for crawl out of the smouldering embers. The clan people ran back, and Tao pointed for all to see. He reached down carefully and picked it up in his hands. It was black and shiny, with bright orange stripes running lengthwise along its back. It walked on four stubby legs. Tiny puffs of steam rose from its fat body.

The clan people and the elders gathered around to see the magic. They gasped in surprise as Wodak told them he saw it crawl right out of the fire. It covered the palm of Tao's hand and sat there, with its tiny eyes bulging in the morning light.

"It is truly magic," said Notar. "We saw it rise up out of the flames."

"It is no bigger than a lizard," Zugor complained.

"It is life, and big enough," said Wodak, glaring at him. "Tao has kept his promise. I saw it with my own eyes. He has brought forth life from fire."

For a moment Tao felt a tinge of guilt. It was nothing but a fire salamander, a common creature that lives most of its life hidden in the moss. It seldom comes into the light of day, but the heat of a fire drives it out into the open. At first Tao thought to tell Wodak and the elders how the trick is done. Then he swallowed hard and remembered what Graybeard always said about the paintings, the amulets, and the healings: "If the people wish to call it magic, then let it be so."

Zugor stood there, his teeth clenched, the anger blazing in his green eyes.

Still smiling, Tao turned to get Deha and Ram, then stopped in shock. They had disappeared. He looked around quickly. Only a moment ago they were standing quietly in the shadows. Now they were gone.

Gardo and the elders shook their heads, surprised. But Wodak stood there, grinning. He pointed down the hill.

There, far below the little camp, they saw Ram leading Deha across the valley. The two made their way slowly along a well-marked trail between the stunted birch trees and waving fields of waist-high grass. Deha held the leash short, while Ram picked his way carefully along the path as if he knew the purpose of the journey—to get Deha away safely.

Tao ran down the slope, through the hemlock forest, dodging around clumps of holly and laurel bushes to catch up to them. Far behind him he could hear Zugor shouting, "A curse on you and your wolf dog! Let the demons of the evil beasts bar your way!"

Tao ran on as the harsh words faded into the distance. The last he heard was "The girl will be back, or I will come and get her. You will see."

Tao closed his ears to the stupid threats and raced on across the meadow. He caught up to Ram and Deha at the river. There he put Deha on the little raft. With the butt end of his spear he poled across to the opposite shore.

Ram paddled along beside them, his head bobbing above the water as he enjoyed his swim.

9

They traveled across the open plains with the sun at their backs. Ram walked slowly, stopping obediently whenever he felt the leash tighten. He led Deha carefully around boulders and fallen logs. She stumbled once or twice as she tripped over a root or a creeper. But each time she did, Ram looked back, waiting until she regained her footing.

Tao walked slightly ahead as they made their way across the grasslands toward the far-distant cliffs. They still had a long way to go, and the boy knew it would be late afternoon before they reached his home in the Land of the Valley People.

Honey buzzards soared in tight circles between clumps of cottony clouds, their open wings dark brown against the pale blue sky. Small flocks of crested larks flew up out of the grass in front of them.

A wagtail circled overhead, singing its happy song, *"Cherweetee cherweetee."*

Deha stopped and looked up, smiling, as if she could see it. "I know that one," she said. "It's brown and yellow, with a black throat and a long tail. I used to see it early in the morning when I went down to the brook for water."

Tao noticed the joy in her face as she remembered, and he wondered how she could still be happy living in the darkness. How bad it must be, he thought, to have seen and now not to see at all. But we will soon be home, and Kala will know how to make her see again.

They came to a long grove of pine trees in the middle of the plains. Tao slowed down, walking carefully, for he knew this area was the stomping grounds of Tonda, the old cow rhino. Here Tonda ranged in and out of the grove, browsing on pine needles and bunchgrass.

The clan hunters knew her well and tried to stay out of her way, for she was a shortsighted, mean-tempered beast. Yet Tao had hunted through these same fields only a short while ago without seeing her, and he hoped he would have such luck again today.

They walked along slowly, the morning sun warming the plains, sending up the sweet smell of new grass. Tao glanced from side to side, watching cautiously. Far on the horizon he could see vultures swooping down onto the plains, and he knew Sandar had made a kill during the night.

They had barely passed the edge of the pine grove

when Tao heard the sound of pounding hooves directly behind them.

Ram turned, growling.

"The earth shakes," said Deha. "What is it?"

Tao looked around quickly. At first he saw only the waves of yellow grass. But he was sure he knew what it was. "Go!" he yelled to Deha. "Keep on going."

Ram bristled.

Tao pointed toward the far-off cliffs. "Go!" he ordered again. "Do not turn back."

Deha pulled the leash taut. Obediently, Ram went on, loping slowly, leading Deha across the open grasslands.

Once again Tao heard the pounding hooves. Quickly he reached into his deerskin pouch and took out his shining stone. Then he turned and stood quietly as Tonda came out of the shadows, snorting and blowing. She came like a great lumbering boulder, the curve of her shoulder higher than Tao's head. Her eyesight was bad, and she lifted her head, sniffing the air. She caught Tao's scent and trotted straight for him, then stopped a stone's throw away.

If Zugor had called up a living demon, thought Tao, he could not have picked a more ornery beast.

Patches of matted hair hung down from her shoulders and under her chest like clumps of moss, and Tao could tell she was shedding her heavy wooly coat of winter. A long curved horn jutted up from the end of her snout. She stood there, stocky and powerful, like a giant boar.

Tao waited, watching her carefully. She stood just outside the pine grove, snorting and pawing at the dirt as if trying to make up her mind.

Step by step, Tao began to back away. But Tonda caught the movement and started for him. She came in a thundering gallop, churning up a cloud of dust.

Quickly Tao held up the shining stone. He caught the bright sunlight on its polished surface and flashed it in her eyes. Abruptly she came to a stop.

Tao held the light steady, keeping her in place while he quickly glanced over his shoulder to be sure Ram and Deha were well out of danger.

Then slowly he backed away again, hoping Tonda would let him go. But he had taken only a few steps, when she charged, head down, ready to trample him into the ground.

Once more Tao flashed the sun in her eyes, and again she stopped, stunned by the brilliant glare. He walked toward her, burning the light into her eyes, driving her back slowly, step by step.

She turned her head from side to side, shying away to get out of the blinding glare. But he held it on her, forcing her back.

Completely baffled now, she lifted her head and snorted in anger. Finally she turned and, with a wheezing grunt, lumbered back into the shadows of the pine grove.

Tao waited a few moments to be sure it was safe. Then slowly he turned and walked away. He looked back once or twice to see her still peering out from between the trees.

When Tao caught up with Deha and Ram, the girl was nervous. "What happened?" she asked.

"It was Tonda, the old rhino," he told her. "She is edgy and quick to charge. I think she will soon have a calf."

Deha sighed. "I remember when she herself was a calf," she said. "I was only a child, and my mother used to take me up on the hill to watch her chase the antelope and reindeer. She was young and playful then. Now that she is older, she is dangerous."

They walked along side by side now, heading for the high cliffs still some distance away.

"Your mother also liked to watch the animals?" asked Tao.

Deha nodded. "She loved the horses and the bison, and whenever she saw the mammoths, her eyes grew wide with wonder. One day she got too close and an old bull trampled her to death."

As they neared the cliffs, small bands of horses raced off in front of them. Far out on the horizon, Tao could see herds of bison and red deer grazing on the shoots of the new spring grass.

By late afternoon they reached the foot of the cliffs, where, high up in the rocks, Tao had a little cave. There he kept special chalks, paints, and sketch stones, and practiced his drawing. He also had stores of dried meats, ground beans, and mushrooms.

Tired and hungry from their long journey, they decided to stop and rest for the night before going on into camp.

Ram went on ahead as Tao guided Deha up the narrow ledge to the cave. Tao started a small fire and prepared a stew from mushrooms and dried antelope meat. It was not much, but it was tasty and served to ease their hunger.

Ram chewed on a fat strip of smoked boar meat while Tao boiled up a skin sack of birch-root tea. This they sipped from small spoonlike mussel shells.

The cave opening was small, but the interior was wide and spacious, with cracks overhead for light to enter. "This is where I stayed when I lived away from the clan," Tao explained.

"Because of the drawings?" asked Deha.

"Yes. At the time I was not a Chosen One, and it was taboo for me to make images. Besides, I had a bad foot and I kept a wolf dog, both of which were taboo." Tao stared into the fire, briefly remembering the good times and the bad. "Graybeard knew I had a great wish to become a cave painter, and he came here often to teach me."

It soon grew dark, and Tao lit a pine torch. Then he walked around the cave, describing the paintings he had made for Graybeard. "Here stands a bison with a great hump on his back, all done in glossy reds and browns. And here an angry boar pig charges across the wall toward a wolf." Then he turned to the opposite wall, and with a glow of pride he held his torch high. "This is my best," he said. "It is Saxon, the sacred bull, the one that almost killed me before I drove him off with the shining stone."

Deha smiled broadly. "I see them in my mind," she said. "How beautiful they are. I only wish I could see them with my eyes."

"You will," said Tao. "Soon now, you will."

From the back of the cave, Tao brought out a smooth, flat slate stone. Deha sat cross-legged on the floor, and Tao placed it in her lap. She brushed it across her cheek, then said quietly, "It is untouched. What is it for?"

"For you," said Tao. "Before you lost your sight you saw many old rhinos. Draw one for me, and I will carry it with my other sketch stones and paint its likeness on the walls of the Secret Caverns."

"You said it is not taboo for a woman to draw on stones," said Deha, "but it is still taboo for a woman to paint on the walls of a cave?"

Tao nodded. "Yes, there are still many taboos, but I do not believe in all of them."

Deha brushed the tips of her fingers over the slate. "It

has been a long time since I saw a beast like Tonda," she said. "But this morning I heard the thunder of her hooves, and once again I see her image in my mind."

Tao gave her the sharpest flint stone he could find, then stepped back and let her work. For a long while he heard her scratching away in the darkness, etching deep into the slate stone, then blowing off the dust. She worked steadily, all the while humming softly, happy in her task.

When she finished, she stood up and handed the stone to Tao. "Now," she said, "quickly, tell me, have I drawn it well and true?"

Tao held his torch up and studied it in the flickering light. He drew in his breath. He had never seen a more perfect sketch. He knew she must see these things clearly in her mind, for it looked as if she had drawn it from life. With one firm, almost unbroken line, she had etched it from the great horn on the snout, over the shoulders and rump, around the legs, and back to the snout again. It was simple, yet bold and strong, with massive shoulders, a piglike snout, and short, sturdy legs.

"It is perfect," he said. "For more than two summers you have not seen a rhino. Yet you remember the actual shape and form of the beast. Every line is exactly right."

Deha smiled, happy that Tao liked it.

"In the summers to come," said Tao, "I will paint it

on the walls of all the Secret Caverns from the valleys to the high mountains, from the lake country to the river cliffs. All the clans will want it."

"And if your Kala can give me back my sight," said Deha, "I will see it all with my own eyes."

10

With the sun already high above the hills, Tao and Deha made their way down the cliff and into the oak woods. Once again, Tao tied Ram to the leash and let him guide Deha along the trail leading to the camp of the Valley People.

Then Tao walked ahead, his deerskin pouch slung over his shoulder, his bad foot curled around the shaft of his spear.

The deep woods rang with the flutelike calls of the golden orioles, while flocks of redstarts darted through the treetops, twittering and flashing their tawny wings.

Even before they reached the camp, they could hear the happy cry of children's voices and the sharp *thwack* of flint axes as the women split wood for the noon fires.

A few moments later they came to the clearing. The smell of roasting acorns filled the air as smoke rose up from around the center of the little camp.

A group of children ran up to greet them. They stared

at Deha, laughing and giggling. One small boy ran ahead, shouting, "It's Tao, Tao is home!" The happy words echoed throughout the camp.

Tao smiled. "It is good to hear my name shouted in welcome," he said, "when only two summers ago, I was an outcast."

"Then it is good to come home?" said Deha.

"Yes," Tao said, "and to see Kala and my people."

The children followed as Tao led Deha into camp.

One by one the women came out of their skin huts to watch them pass. Deha sensed the excitement. She held her head high, pushing her long dark hair back from her forehead and tossing it over her shoulder. She stepped spryly, holding on to Tao's arm as they walked along.

Tao heard gasps and murmurs from some of the clan women peering through the trees. They nodded to one another and covered their mouths with their hands, as if they knew a secret.

Tao brought Deha directly to Kala's hut. He stood outside and called softly, "Kala, it is I, Tao."

A moment later the skin flap opened and Kala emerged with a child in her arms. Her dark hair hung down over her plump face in long strings. She shifted the baby into her left arm, then grinned and threw the other arm around Tao, slapping him on the back roughly. She spoke in a deep throaty voice. "So, you are back and you are well," she said, all in one breath. "That is good."

Then she saw Deha and her grin became a big smile. "Ah-ha, best of all you bring home a mate. From where? From the Land of the Mountain People, yes? They have the fair ones." She laughed knowingly and jabbed Tao in the ribs with her elbow. "Maybe you steal her the way your father stole your mother?"

Tao shook his head and forced a smile, glancing around at the staring eyes of the women. "No," he hastened to explain, "it is not like that. Deha is a friend, a friend from across the river." He took Deha's arm and gently turned her toward Kala. "Deha lives in darkness," he said. "You see, she is blind." He took a deep breath and went on: "I know you have special herbs and oils for curing. I brought her to you so you could heal her and make her see again."

Kala looked at the boy, a strained expression on her face. She studied Deha for a moment, gazing intently into her dark eyes. She passed her hand in front of the girl's face. Then she sighed deeply and shook her head. She stooped down and opened the flap of the hut. "Go in, child," she said, "go in."

After Deha entered the hut, Kala turned and glared back at Tao. She clicked her tongue the way she always did when she was annoyed. "I will speak with you later," she said. She closed the flap in his face and left him standing there, with all the clan people looking on.

Tao shrugged. Then, with Ram at his heels, he started through the camp toward his father's hut. On the way he let Ram off the leash. The children gathered around the wolf dog, pushing and shoving to get close. They reached out and giggled as his cold nose nuzzled their hands and faces.

Tao left him to play with the children and walked across the clearing. He passed an old woman sitting under an elm tree, chewing on an otter pelt to soften it before sewing it into a pair of sandals. Farther on an elderly man bent over a tree stump, carefully binding a new spearhead to a shaft of ironwood.

Tao had almost reached the center of camp when he saw Volt, his father, coming toward him. The big leader walked tall and straight, his dark blue eyes squinting from long summers of hunting on the open plains.

Tao's body stiffened, for although they were friends, they often quarreled, and the boy was never quite sure what to expect.

Still, Volt was the clan leader, and Tao greeted him with respect. He noticed some gray streaks in his father's hair, and the scars on his cheek were partially hidden by new wrinkles. Yet it was good to see him looking as strong as ever with his brawny arms and his heavy wolverine cloak thrown over his shoulder.

The big man planted himself in the boy's path and looked down at him with a stern expression. "We see little of you these days," he said, "now that you travel from clan to clan."

Tao shrugged. He knew his father was right. He had

been away most of the winter, painting and drawing in the Secret Caverns. He bit his lip, then said, "When the season of rituals is over, perhaps I can come back more often." But even as he said it, he realized it sounded like a poor excuse.

Volt shook his head, rattling the bear-claw necklace around his neck. "I thought, now that the girl is here, you might stay."

Tao smiled uneasily and explained about Deha. "As soon as her eyes are healed, she will go back to her people."

"It would be better if she stays here and you stay with her," said Volt as he scratched his cheek with his big hand and glanced around the camp. "I think the spirits would like that."

The familiar knot of anger churned in Tao's stomach. He respected his father as a leader, but he knew, like most of the other clan people, he still believed in the old ways and the old taboos.

The big man stood there, towering over the boy like a shaggy giant, a frown on his face. "You were named painter of the Valley People, not painter of all the clans."

Tao winced. He was sorry he could not always do as his father wished, but this urge to paint and to travel was strong in him. He sighed, stared at the ground, and said nothing.

Volt grunted and shook his head. "So go," he said, "go if you must. But someday, when you grow tired of this wandering, maybe you will come home and help with the hunting." With that he turned and walked away.

Tao stood for a moment, waiting for his anger to subside. Then he went over to the cook fires and begged some deer meat and duck eggs from one of the women. He sat down near the big fire in the center of camp. Ram came over, and they shared the meat and eggs between them. After the meal Tao chewed on a handful of hazelnuts. Then he rested and watched the children playing at their games.

The boys threw spears made from reeds, seeing who could throw the farthest. The girls ran about, chasing one another, holding deer antlers over their heads. For a while Ram lay curled up at Tao's feet, fast asleep.

It was almost dark when Kala came out of her hut. She plopped herself down beside the boy, and from the way she chewed on her spruce gum, Tao knew she was angry.

She spat into the fire. Then, without looking at Tao, she said, "This poor girl, what did you tell her?"

Tao flinched, not knowing what she meant. "I told her you would be able to make her see again."

Kala spat into the fire again, and a small shower of sparks flew up. "And how will I make her see?" She threw up her hands. "With what? With magic, with the eye of a frog, with the blood of a snake, with sticks in the dirt? How? Tell me how."

Tao swallowed hard. He could think of nothing to

say. Then he blurted out, "But, but you know the plants, the things Graybeard taught you, the things from the earth, the berries, the roots that cure. Many times I have seen you use them."

"And what did you see, eh? What? You saw me stop a fever with the root of the hooded plant. You saw me wrap the leaves of the plantain around your cuts and bruises. You saw me take away a headache with the tea of the cherry bark."

"Even more," Tao said.

Kala shook her head. "Ach, these things are nothing, nothing at all, a toothache, a gnashed finger, nothing." She glared at the boy in the darkness. "I cannot cure blindness. Do you understand? I am not a maker of magic or a sorcerer or any of those wishful things. I am only Kala the medicine woman. I talk to no spirits or demons. I can do only what the earth and the plants will let me do—nothing more."

There was a long silence as Tao sat speechless, staring into the fire. His eyes burned, and he rubbed them with the backs of his hands.

Kala cleared her throat and turned to Tao, and he could tell she also felt bad. "How did this blindness happen?" she asked quietly.

"Deha fell from a bee tree two summers ago while collecting honey. When they found her she could not see. Zugor the mad Neander says she is possessed by demons. I do not believe that. But I thought you would have a special root or herb to make her see again."

Kala sighed. She reached over, crooked her finger under Tao's chin, and turned his face up to look at her. "Tao, listen to me," she said. "Blindness is more than a pain in the belly. It is more than a sting of a bee or a sore finger. It is something deep in the head, a thing I do not know about." She threw up her hands again. "So I can do nothing."

Tao groaned. "Does that mean Deha will have to go back to her cave?"

She stared at Tao blankly. Her mouth dropped open. "What cave?"

"In the mountains," he said. "Zugor keeps her in a cave to protect the Mountain People from her demons."

"The girl is kept in a cave?"

"Yes," said Tao, "in a cave with the Evil Children."

Kala got to her feet, her voice rasping with anger. "And what does this fool say is wrong with the children?"

"He says they are possessed of evil spirits like Deha. I saw them. They are weak. Their heads fall on their chests, and their arms are thin and crooked like the branches of the oak tree."

Kala paced up and down. She stared off toward the distant mountains, her arms folded over her chest. "He keeps them in a cave. Then how do they live?"

"Jema brings them earth apples and ground beans left over from the cook fires."

"Nothing else?"

Tao shook his head.

Kala was quiet for a moment. Only the sound of the night breeze rustling through the oak trees broke the silence. Then she asked, "How long have they been like this?"

"Since the summer before last, I think."

The old woman nodded. "That was the summer of the long dryness, when the herds did not come back and food was scarce."

"Yes," said Tao.

"Hmm." Kala pursed her lips. "We had some children like that many years ago. Yes, I remember now. Graybeard went on a long journey and brought back leaves and a strange meat to cure them." She stood for a moment, thinking. "He left an antelope pelt with drawing on it, showing where the medicine can be found."

Tao jumped to his feet. "You have it?"

"It is hidden," said Kala.

Excitement welled up within him. "Then you will show me where it is?"

Kala looked at him for a long time, tapping her finger against her cheek. "We will see," she said. "We will see."

"Just think," Tao said, "if I can find the medicine, then maybe we can cure the children—and Deha, too."

"You see, for you, right away the thing is done." Kala clicked her tongue. "I said nothing about curing the blindness."

"It is my fault," Tao said. "I promised too much. Now what will I tell her?"

"Never mind," said Kala. "I will tell her in my own way. She can stay with me. Here she can live with the clan. Besides, she is already taking care of the little one, the new orphan."

"The Mountain People will be fearful," Tao said. "Zugor told them that if Deha does not return, her demons will seek out another member of the clan."

"Bah," said Kala, spitting in the dirt. "Let the wild man rage. Some day the Mountain People will find out that Neanders are harmless and Zugor nothing but a noisy old goat. Then they will ignore him."

Tao looked up quickly. "Kala, are there many Neanders still left in the mountains?"

Kala smiled. "In the mountains, in the lake country, everywhere there are some, but not many. They come from long ago. They have strange ways, so the clan people shun them and are afraid."

Kala went back to her hut, and Tao sat in the darkness, thinking about what she had said.

A bright yellow moon moved slowly across the purple sky, while Tao heard Sandar roar down in the valley. He knew that the big lion and his mates were already out on the hunt.

Later he heard the soft notes of Deha's flute. He had no way of knowing what Kala told her, but he felt sure it was her way of forgetting her disappointment. At least here she could live with Kala and make her drawings without fear.

Soon many of the clan people gathered around outside the hut, dancing and swaying to the joyful notes of Deha's music.

Tao smiled. He knew the people had already accepted her into the clan.

11

That night Tao slept by the fire, huddling close to Ram to keep himself warm. He awoke to the sound of children playing and the clan women bringing in wood to start the cook fires.

An eagle owl hooted from the deep spruce woods, and high overhead a string of geese honked and called as they made their way toward some distant lake.

Tao ate a chunk of dried venison and a handful of hazelnuts while he waited for Kala. When he saw her come out of her hut, he ran to her. "Today you will show me where the medicine is found?"

Kala frowned and looked at the sky. "The sun is barely up and already you are in a hurry." She glanced around the sleepy camp at the few clan women already busy tending the fires, getting ready for the morning meal. "Come along, then," she said. "Follow me."

Kala carried a deerskin bag over her shoulder as she led Tao up through the oak wood. The boy vaulted along behind her, his bad leg wrapped around the shaft of his spear.

A morning dew covered the ground. Everything smelled fresh and damp. A pair of ravens cawed, scolding from high in the treetops as Kala and the boy made their way silently up the gentle slope, stepping over stones and fallen logs all covered with moss.

Deep in the woods Kala stopped. She bent down and searched around one of the logs. She turned it over and caught a lizard, still sluggish from the morning chill. She killed it with a stick and put it in her bag.

At the foot of an old oak tree she poked at a little plant. "Look," she said, "see the small blue flowers, the way the leaves lie across the ground in runners?"

Tao nodded as she dug it out with her fingers, roots and all, and held it up for him to see. She shook it gently to remove the dirt. "This one is good for healing," she said. "The roots you mash on a stone, then boil until the water is white. Let it cool, and drink it with the tea of the birch tree."

Tao waited eagerly. This was the kind of thing he wanted to learn. "Will this cure the children?"

Kala shook her head, annoyed at his impatience. "No . . . no . . . no, it is only to stop a fever or ease a pain in the head." She glanced around again. "Come," she said.

They went up beyond the oak wood to the foot of the cliffs, where the huge boulders stood like great herds of stone mammoths. They walked into the middle, where the giant stones towered all around them.

Kala counted each one as she passed. Then she stopped and peered into a crack in one of the rocks. She slipped her hand into the narrow crevice and felt around inside. She pulled her arm out empty-handed and tried again, lower down.

Tao watched as she reached deep into the opening.

"Ah," she whispered, "here it is, still safe and dry." She brought out a roll of birch bark tied together with a leather thong. She opened it and unrolled an antelope pelt almost as long as her arm.

It was the hide of a newborn calf, with the furry side as soft and downy as a milkweed leaf. The other side was clean and smooth and covered with strange markings, simple sketches of animals, plants, and birds all etched into the hide with a burning stick.

"This is the drawing I told you about," said Kala. "It tells where the medicine is. But to find it you must first understand what it means."

"Why do you hide it?"

Kala shrugged. "When he was ill and knew he was dying, Graybeard told me to keep it safe, to give it only to someone I could trust, someone of good sense." She held it out to Tao. "I have thought about it long and hard, and I knew that when the time was right that person would be you."

Tao took it in his hands and studied it, puzzled by the

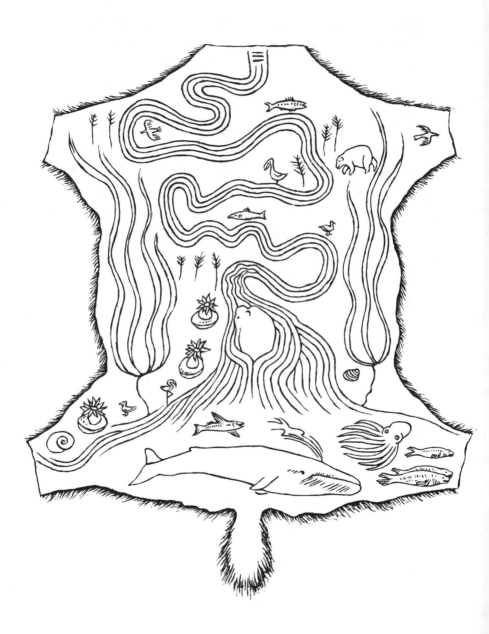

strange images. Three short bars appeared at the top, followed by four long lines that curved and turned all the way down the entire length of the hide. Narrow ribbon-shaped leaves and large shells with delicate-looking flowers decorated the margins of the pelt.

Tao stared at it for a while, then shook his head. "What does it mean? Where is the medicine?"

"That is how Graybeard made it," said Kala. "It must mean something. He was wise enough to choose you as Cave Painter. Now maybe you will be wise enough to see what he is trying to tell us."

Tao studied it again, trying to make sense of it. A large drawing of a gigantic fish spitting water from the top of its head filled the lower margin of the pelt. Just above that was the sketch of another fish flying through the air like a bird. Three strange animals without legs lay in one corner next to what looked like a head with big eyes and many arms.

The longer Tao pondered it, the more bewildering it became. "It tells me nothing," he said. "So how will I find the medicine?"

"Slowly," said Kala, "slowly. Do not be in such a hurry. Go somewhere, sit quietly and study the pictures. Think about them. Maybe they will speak to you." She frowned at him and clicked her tongue. Then she turned and walked away, leaving him with the annoying puzzle.

Tao heard her parting words: "Young ones," she

mumbled, "like yearling colts, galloping off in all directions, going no place in a hurry."

Tao waited until she disappeared through the oak trees. Then he rolled up the pelt and tucked it under his belt. Deep in thought, he climbed up the steep slope toward the cliffs. On the way he thought he saw a fleeting shadow dart between the boulders. It glided silently like a gray ghost, then disappeared. He waited a moment, listening, but heard only the rustling of the oak leaves. He shrugged and went on, certain that it was only his imagination.

When he came to the foot of the cliffs, he started up the narrow ledge. He climbed slowly, watching his footing around the stunted pine trees growing in the middle of the path. He reached the top, and then looked out across the valley to see the open plains and the slough with the winding river running behind it. As a boy he often sat here and watched the bison grazing on the bunchgrass, and sometimes he was lucky enough to see the lumbering herds of mammoths when they migrated across the valley.

He sat now with his legs dangling over the edge of the cliff, and he saw scattered bands of horses grazing across the grasslands.

Then, carefully, he unrolled the antelope pelt and spread it out on his lap. He ran his finger from top to bottom over the long winding lines, trying to understand what they meant. He kept turning it around this way and that to be sure which was the top and which was the bottom. Yet as hard as he tried, he still could not make much sense of it.

Crude images of fish, birds, and trees filled in along the edges of the curving lines like markers on a trail. Halfway down, an object stood in the middle like a frozen mammoth.

Tao turned the pelt around again, but then all the fish were upside down and the birds were flying with their feet up, so he knew the first way must be right.

Time and again he looked at it, running his finger over the drawings, searching for a sign or a clue. The margins of the pelt, with the sketches of the long flat leaves, the shells, and the delicate flowers, were beautifully drawn. But were they only ornaments, or were they a part of the puzzle? He could not tell.

He got up, stretched, and shook his head. He would have to tell Kala it was no use, he still could not understand what Graybeard was trying to say.

He started to leave, when he heard someone coming. He looked down and blinked, hardly daring to believe what he saw. There was Deha, with Ram leading her up the narrow ledge. Step by step she climbed, leaning against the cliff, feeling her way along.

Tao held his breath as he watched her squeeze between the stunted pines, her feet getting close to the edge. She stopped once or twice to keep her balance, then went on.

Tao said nothing until she reached the top. Then he reached out and pulled her up onto the cliff beside him. "Are you mad?" he asked. "You walk in darkness, like a blind ibex. One slip and you would fall to the rocks below."

Deha grinned. "I feel safe with Ram," she said. "He knows the trails well and would not let me fall. Besides, Kala said I should come and help you with the puzzle."

Tao groaned. "Yes, but Kala did not know I was sitting on top of the cliffs. If you had eyes you would know it is a long way down."

Tao made the girl sit away from the edge of the cliff. He stood beside her and unrolled the pelt once more.

"I can tell you what the drawings are," he said. "But without sight how can you know what it means?"

"Tell me anyway," said Deha.

Tao described the pelt with its strange images and drawings. He finished by saying, "There are animals like fat badgers without legs, and a head with eight arms." Tao sighed. "All morning I have studied it and still it tells me nothing."

"Do you think Graybeard would make drawings that are not true?" said Deha.

"A fish that flies and one that spits water out of the top of its head?" asked Tao. "These are beasts I have never seen or heard of before. Maybe they are the demons that Zugor speaks of."

"What about the leaves?" asked Deha.

"Yes," said the boy, "long narrow leaves on each side of the pelt, and shells with flowers growing on top."

Deha shook her head. "Nothing else?"

"Nothing," said Tao. "Nothing, except the long wavy lines running all the way down to the bottom of the pelt."

"Wavy lines?" said Deha. "That sounds like water."

Tao was staring out over the valley. The wide expanse of open plains lay below, with the slough off to one side. Behind it the river meandered through the grasslands in great curves. The sun glinted off its surface like dots of fire, turning it into a winding, golden path.

Tao glanced down at the pelt again. From where he was standing, the wavy lines on the drawing matched the course of the river. Every turn, every bend flowed exactly as shown on the pelt. How had he missed it? Even the three short lines at the top began to make sense.

"You are right," he said. "The wavy lines are the water; the water is the river." He rubbed his fingers over the pelt as if it were a magic thing. He reached down and pulled Deha to her feet. "Come," he said excitedly, "we must tell Kala."

Then he wrapped his bad foot around the shaft of his spear and hobbled down the narrow ledge, guiding

Deha along carefully behind him. Ram loped on ahead as they made their way through the oak-wood forest and on into camp.

Tao stopped in front of Kala's hut, panting and out of breath.

"Kala!" he called. "Kala!"

The old woman came out. She saw Tao smiling. "You found where the medicine is?" she asked.

The boy unrolled the pelt and held it up. "Yes," he said. "Deha found the water, and now we know what it means." He pointed to the lines. "Look, here is the river, the wavy lines." Then he pointed to the three short marks at the top. "And this is a raft. Graybeard is telling me to go downriver."

Kala nodded. "All right, that's good," she said. "But where is the medicine?"

Tao hesitated. "I, I don't know yet. I only know this is where I start. I will go downriver and follow the drawings on the pelt until I find the medicine."

They sat on the ground under the big oak tree, Kala on one side of Tao, and Deha on the other.

From high in the tree a carrion crow called, *haw, haw . . . haw, haw.*

Kala looked up, a half smile on her face. "You see, even the crow knows you are mad. You go running off like a scared rabbit, this way and that, not even knowing what to look for."

Tao pointed to the picture of the fish spouting water.

"It is somewhere down here, I know it, near the end of the river."

Kala stared at the pelt. She tilted her head to one way, then the other. "Ah," she said, "you know where that is?"

"No," said Tao, shaking his head.

"That is the Land of the Great Waters."

Tao slapped his hand against his thigh. "Yes, now I remember. The Land of the Great Waters," he repeated under his breath. "Graybeard told me of such a place."

"When I was only a child," said Kala, "three of our hunters went there."

"Then tell us," said Deha, "what did they find?"

Kala shook her head sadly. "Only one came back. That was Graybeard. He told us of strange animals and a great fish as big and as fat as a mountain." Kala stared into the distance. "It is a long journey," she said, "three days beyond the slough."

Tao still had the pelt open on his lap. He jumped up and pointed to the three marks at the top. "Then I will take my raft and go downriver faster than a man can walk."

Deha nodded, a big smile on her face. "And I will go with you."

Tao frowned. "No," he said, shaking his head. "You cannot see."

"But I can paddle," said Deha. "I can fish and cook and tie knots and help in many ways."

"No," Kala said, "Tao is right. Without sight it would be too dangerous."

Deha sighed. "How many strange things you will see," she said. "If only I had eyes to go with you."

"Tomorrow," said Tao, "I will leave early. I must travel quickly and come back soon if I am to help the children."

Kala got up. She put her hands on her hips. "I know I am a fool," she said, "but if I don't help you, you will go anyway. So I will give you what you need: grass rope, skin sacks, dried meat, and new sandals. The rest you will have to find along the way."

Kala and Deha went back to their hut, and Tao stood there for a while, thinking about the journey. Then, as he turned to go, he saw a ghostlike figure disappear into the darkness of the hemlock trees. It was hunched over, with long gray hair flying out behind it. Tao peered into the shadows but saw only the branches of the trees swaying in the breeze. Is it Zugor? he wondered. Then he shrugged. Perhaps it is only a clan woman gathering mushrooms.

12

The next morning Tao brought Ram up to Kala's hut. The old woman sat under the big hickory tree, feeding the baby a meal made of ground beans and acorn pulp. Deha sat beside them, cutting strips of dried venison for the next meal.

As he came closer, Tao put the wolf dog on the leash and handed the other end to Deha. "Keep Ram with you," he said. "He knows you well and will protect you."

At first Deha shook her head no. Then quickly she changed her mind. "Perhaps you are right," she said. "He can be my eyes and guide me safely while you are gone."

Kala said little as the boy made ready to go.

Tao slung the long coil of grass rope over his shoulder, along with the extra skin sacks that Kala had made for him with which to bring back plants, herbs, and other medicines that he might find. He took along some slates and chalks for drawing, then turned and squeezed Kala's arm, thanking her for all her help.

The old woman wiped her eyes with the back of her hand. "Go, now," she said. "Be careful, and do nothing foolish. Find your medicine and come back quickly."

Then, with the antelope pelt, his flint ax, and his knife tucked under his belt, Tao walked down the hill and out across the plains toward the river.

He walked cautiously through the waist-high grass, looking about for lurking hyenas or leopards, for he did not have Ram now to warn him of danger.

When he reached the river, Tao found his little raft snagged under the overhanging willow branches where he had left it. It was still intact, but two of the logs were coming loose. If he wanted to go far downriver, he would need to tighten them and add another log or two to make the raft larger. Sturdy oak and willow trees covered the banks, but he had not the time to cut them down with his small hand ax.

Instead, he found a number of fallen pine logs of just the right length lying on the hillside between the shrubs and laurel bushes. He lopped off the branches and dragged the logs down to the bank. There, on a level stretch of the beach, he laid them lengthwise beside the raft. When he had them all in place, he dug up long strings of tough cedar roots and lengths of greenbrier vines. He laced these back and forth between the logs, pulling them snug, binding them tightly together.

Next he cut a stake of birch wood about waist high and with a heavy stone he pounded it upright between the logs. This made a center post on which to tie his belongings or to balance himself. In the same way, he wedged a short stake between the logs near the front of the raft to haul it upstream or to tie it to the bank at night.

He worked all afternoon until it began to grow dark. Then he walked along the shore turning over half-submerged rocks, where he caught a few little darters about the size and shape of his thumb. He speared these on long willow sticks and roasted them over a fire, along with a few mushrooms that he had found on the stump of an old swamp oak.

The next morning he took all his belongings, his firestones, the large skin sacks, some chalks, and drawing slates, and placed them in the center of the raft, along with his spear and his coil of grass rope. His flint knife he tucked under his belt; his shining stone he kept in his deerskin pouch slung over his shoulder.

With that ready he waded downstream, hobbling along the bank to the nearest birch woods, where he cut a long straight pole. He spent time pruning off the sprigs and shoots until it was clean and smooth. Then he turned and waded back upstream. He had almost reached the raft when he heard a screeching howl come from the woods nearby.

Still knee-deep in water, he stopped. His spear lay on

the raft a short distance away, so he held up his hand ax and waited.

A moment later Ram came barging out of the underbrush, with Deha close behind him, holding the other end of the leash. Tao stood in disbelief as the wolf dog led the girl out onto the raft then stood beside her with his tail wagging and his pink tongue lolling out of the side of his mouth.

Once again the howling scream came from out of the woods.

Deha cringed. "Tao, are you there?" she called.

"Yes," said Tao. "What happened?"

"It is Zugor," the girl said. "He follows me."

"Then why did you leave the camp?"

"To go with you."

Tao shook his head. "You cannot come with me. You know that."

"But I told you, I can help," said Deha. "I can paddle. I can fish and cook."

Tao pointed off toward the plains. "No," he said firmly, "you must go back. Let Ram take you, now."

Deha had found the post in the middle of the raft. She held on to it as if afraid of being forced to go. "I will not be in the way," she said. "I can help you find the medicine."

Tao shook his head again. "No, you cannot see, and I have not the time to take care of you."

Just then the howling scream came again, this time closer.

"It's Zugor," said Deha. "He comes to beat me with a switch and drive out my demons."

"Then go back now," said Tao. "Ram will not let him hurt you."

Deha shivered. "Ram is brave, but Zugor shakes a fetish in his face and drives him off."

"What fetish?"

"The stench of the polecat," said Deha. "Ram hates it and runs away."

She had barely spoken when the shrill cry came again. Tao heard a movement in the underbrush. At the same time he caught a strong whiff of the nauseating odor. Quickly he jumped aboard the raft. With his long pole he pushed it off the beach and out into the river.

A moment later Zugor jumped from the bushes, swinging a dead polecat over his head. In his other hand he held a stout willow switch. "Let the girl go," he screamed. "It is time to punish her evil spirits."

"Go back to your mountains," Tao shouted. "The girl stays here with me." He held his nose against the sickening odor.

Zugor laughed, a wild, hysterical giggle, "Tee-hee-hee-hee, tee-hee-hee." In a shrill voice he yelled, "The demons are waiting for you, wherever you go—waiting to get you, tee-hee-hee." He splashed into the water, chasing after the raft, swinging the dead polecat around his head.

Deha huddled on the raft, clasping her arms tightly around the center post. Ram stood on the far end, snorting against the evil smell.

Tao jammed the long pole into the river bottom and pushed the raft farther out. He grimaced as the sickening odor of the polecat reached him.

Zugor flung the polecat out over the water. The long brown-and-white, rabbit-sized body flew through the air and landed on the raft. Quickly Tao flipped it into the river with the end of his pole.

Zugor laughed again, "Haw-haw-haw." He ran along the riverbank, following the raft as it drifted slowly downstream. His dirty long hair hung down to his knees, covering his entire body. He was rawboned and gaunt, but he ran and jumped, as nimble as an old mountain goat.

"The blind one," he shouted, "she still cannot see, can she? I knew it, I knew it. She is still possessed. You see, you see, your medicine woman knows nothing about the spirits."

The swirling waters carried the raft along slowly, and Zugor kept up for a short distance, pushing his way through the reeds, splashing through the shallows, shaking his fist over his head. "The river demons will get you," he cried. "They will follow you to the Great

Waters. There the giant fish will drag you down into the deep, tee-hee-hee."

Laughing like a hyena, the old man skipped and danced along the bank, and Tao remembered the fleeting gray ghost he had seen disappearing into the shadows. Now he was certain it had been Zugor snooping, listening to everything he said.

The dead polecat floated along beside them, and Tao pushed harder to get away from the putrid odor and the old man's annoying threats. As the raft swept downstream, Tao heard the last of the wild curses echo faintly across the water. "Even if you find the medicine, it will do no good," the old man shouted. "You do not know the magic . . . the magic . . . the magic . . . tee-hee-hee."

The current carried them along faster and faster. Ram stood near the front, watching the long-legged herons and the big white storks fly up as the raft moved toward them.

Tao glanced back at Deha. "We will stop just beyond the slough," he said. "The madman is far away now, and Ram can lead you back to camp."

Deha frowned. "I promise I will not be in the way," she pleaded. "Besides, I have never been to such a wonderful place as the Great Waters before."

Tao pushed hard with his pole, sending the raft surging ahead. "But you cannot see. Of what use is it?"

"Then you will be my eyes," said Deha. "I can smell

and hear and feel, and you can tell me everything you see."

"It is dangerous," said Tao. "I don't even know what lies beyond the slough, and there are strange beasts, maybe more fierce than anything we have ever seen."

"Like the fish as big as a mountain?" said Deha.

"That and more," said Tao.

Deha was quiet for a moment as she groped around with her hands. Then she found the spear lying on the damp logs. She grabbed it, stood up, and made her way cautiously to the edge of the raft.

Tao felt the raft careen ahead. He looked around and saw the girl poling with the butt end of the spear.

"See," said Deha, "I told you I could help, that I would not be in the way."

Tao sighed in resignation.

A warm morning sun beat down, and beads of perspiration ran down Tao's face and chest as he pushed hard with the pole to steer between sandbars and protruding logs.

The river widened now. It swerved and turned in great sweeps, meandering first one way then the other. It flowed slowly through the slough, where water rails clattered and squawked in the tall rushes. Coots and moorhens scampered away in front of them and disappeared into the reeds.

They drifted across the open plains, where the river was placid and the greenish-brown water swirled all around them. Far in the distance Tao could see mixed herds of saiga antelope and bison grazing on the new spring grasses. Skeins of geese and white swans passed high overhead, honking and trumpeting as they headed for the distant lakes.

Tao and Deha pushed with their poles, sending the raft speeding downriver.

"Kala said it was a three days' walk to the Great Waters," said Deha, "but this is much easier than walking."

"And faster," said Tao. "We should reach the Great Waters before dark."

Ram stood near the front of the raft. He growled and snarled when he saw fat sows with litters of piglets rooting along the banks, and families of otters splashing and playing in the shallows.

Once past the plains, they sailed between high mountains of hemlock and spruce with thickets of birch and alder growing down to the water's edge. Great masses of rock lined the shores.

Then the current picked up, racing, tumbling faster and faster. In places the river rushed between huge boulders, creating whirlpools of white water.

Tao jammed his pole against the rocks to keep from crashing into them. It was hard to keep the raft steady now. They bounced up and down, buffeted from side to side by the churning waters. The clumsy craft pitched and tossed as it rushed headlong into the boiling cataracts.

Tao stared ahead, blinking his eyes against the wind-blown spray, surprised by the roaring, plunging waters in front of him. He tried to steer, but the raft spun around like a chip of wood in a swirling torrent. Smashing waves crashed against the rocks, sending up clouds of mist.

These must be the river demons Zugor warned of, Tao thought. He spread out his feet to keep his balance and shouted to Deha, "Quick, grab hold of the center post!"

Deha tucked the spear under the sacks and coils of rope, then braced herself as the raft plunged into the rapids.

The roar of the water rang in their ears as huge waves crashed over them, drenching them in clouds of spray. The raft spun around, plunging from one whirlpool to another.

Deha stretched out on her stomach, clinging to the center post. Ram lay flat with his legs splayed out.

Unable to keep his feet, Tao threw himself down beside the girl. He grabbed on to the center post with his left hand. With his right hand he held on to the scruff of Ram's neck to keep him from being washed overboard. Down, down they plunged as the raft lurched and rolled. Tao hung on tightly, gritting his teeth against the jolting ride.

He turned and suddenly realized Deha was no longer with him. Glancing back he saw her slipping away, her hands clawing and grasping at the wet logs. He stretched out his legs as far as he could and shouted over the roar of the water, "Grab on to my foot, my ankle, anything!"

Tao hung on, waiting. Then out of the corner of his eye he saw Deha groping for a handhold to pull herself up. She reached out, and her fingers grasped the end of the grass rope lying across the raft.

"No, not that," Tao shouted, "not that!"

But even as he spoke he knew it was too late. Deha slipped off the raft and beneath the waves with the rope in her hand, dragging most of their belongings with her, including Tao's drawing slates, his sacks and firc-stones. Tao lay there, straining his neck, glancing back, searching, but all he could see was the tumbling waves and the crashing spray of white water.

He could not get to his feet, so he waited, trying to catch his breath. How long he lay there, he did not know, but slowly he realized the raft was drifting quietly. The roaring sound of the cataracts had died away. Tao stood as the raft moved along in a wide channel of calm water. Quickly he looked back. At first he saw only the swirling current winding its way behind him. Then, in the distance, he noticed a dark brown object bobbing on the water. He picked up his pole and jammed it into the sandy bottom, stopping the raft. He looked again as the object came closer, and he gasped. It was Deha, drifting along with the current, keeping herself afloat by clinging to the coil of rope.

Tao reached out with the pole. "Deha, I'm right in front of you! Grab hold of the pole!"

Gasping and spitting water, Deha reached for the pole until she found it, and Tao pulled her aboard. She sat on the wet logs, with her arms around her knees, breathing hard. "I'm sorry," she said. "I came along to help, not to be in the way."

Tao grimaced. "How can you help when you cannot see? The Great Waters are no place for a blind girl. I should have made you go back before," he groaned. "Now it's too late." His hands reached around to be sure his skin pouch with his shining stone was still safe and that the antelope pelt and his flint knife were still tucked under his belt.

Tight-lipped and glum, Deha sat in silence as Tao silently poled the raft ahead.

Before them the river washed between narrow channels of spits and sandbars. Here the water was shallow, and Tao easily guided the raft around the twists and turns of the channel.

They sailed on for most of the afternoon with a cold silence between them. Tao took the antelope pelt from his belt and spread it out on the wet logs. He followed the wavy lines with his finger, tracing them down past the rapids to where the waters spread out like the branches of a tree. He smiled. It is not far, he thought. We will reach the Great Waters before darkness.

Glints of silver flashed in the late-afternoon sun.

"Salmon," cried Tao, "on their way far upstream to the shallows. Soon the clan people will eat well."

Then he gasped in surprise. All around them, big brown bears stood on the sandbars or hip-deep in water, scooping out the wriggling fish or grabbing them in their jaws to carry them up on the banks, where they tore them apart, eating as many as they could catch.

Deha sensed Tao's excitement. In spite of her ruffled feelings, she could not contain her curiosity. "What is it?" she asked.

"Bears," said Tao, "fishing for salmon. More bears than I have ever seen before."

They drifted on swiftly. At first Tao could barely make out anything against the glare of the sun. Then, just ahead, he saw where the river branched out into many channels. He balanced himself and glanced at the antelope pelt, holding it down with his feet. He studied the lines near the bottom of the pelt, but he could not tell which way to go.

Faster and faster they swept along. Tao stood up on his toes, staring ahead, trying to make up his mind.

Then a huge stone rose up in the middle of the channel, off to the right. It looked like an old gray mammoth. Tao glanced down and saw it on the pelt—the image of the mammoth. Yet they were already heading in the wrong direction.

13

The raft lunged ahead, swept along by the strong current. Quickly Tao plunged his pole into the water. He felt it sink into the soft mud, and he pushed hard, straining with all his might to force the raft over into the right channel.

Now, in the midst of their troubles, Tao and Deha forgot their quarrel. Deha picked up the spear to help.

"Quick," shouted Tao, "the other way, the other way."

Deha tried, but the spear would not touch bottom. The water was too deep.

The raft hung for a moment, motionless, as if held in place. Tao pushed and shoved, but nothing happened. He groaned. The pole was stuck fast in the mud. He tried again, pulling hard. It would not budge.

Deha dropped the spear and moved over beside him. She reached out, groping. Together they pulled and tugged to wrench it free. They rocked it back and forth, but it would not come loose.

Just then a swirl of current caught the raft and it burst ahead. Tao grit his teeth and tried to hang on, but little by little, the wet pole slipped through his hands and the raft swung free. Now, drifting out of control, they plunged forward. With a harsh scraping sound and a thud, they slammed into a hidden rock.

Tao and the girl stumbled backward and fell, the wind knocked out of them. There they lay on their backs, watching the clouds turn as the raft spun around in the swirling current. Ram sprawled beside them, clawing at the wet logs to keep from falling overboard.

Slowly Tao got to his feet. He looked up to see the big rock like a gray mammoth standing in the middle of the stream, just as it showed on the antelope pelt. They passed close beside it. Tao grinned. "We sail in the right channel," he shouted.

"Graybeard brings us luck," said Deha, getting up. She sniffed the air. "It smells fresh and salty."

They sailed through vast fields of reeds that stretched away on all sides as far as Tao could see. Birds were everywhere, swimming and flying around the raft. Tao watched in amazement as sea gulls, ducks, and pelicans swooped and dived over his head. Many of the birds he had seen back home around the big lakes. But many were strange, like the ducks with the bright red heads, and the long-legged birds with the curved bills.

Tao found all of these things marked on the pelt, and

he realized that every sketch, every picture was a sign
he was to follow on his way to find the medicine.

Once beyond the reeds the raft sped along faster and
faster. Tao tried to guide it with his spear, but the water
was far too deep. Now they could only drift wherever
the current would take them, and it carried them far
into the biggest lake Tao had ever seen.

A bright orange sun hovered just above the water,
glinting off the waves. Here and there, small patches of
brown weed drifted by.

"This is it," said Tao. "This must be the Great Waters."

Deha stood up in the center of the raft, holding on to
the post. "Tell me what you see," she said. "What is it
like?"

Just then a fish leaped out of the water. It spread its
wings and skimmed over the waves like a bird.

"There," said Tao, "there goes the fish that flies. Just
the way Graybeard drew it on the pelt." He looked
around. "There's another," he shouted, "and another, all
silver and shiny in the sunlight."

Deha took a deep breath. "How wonderful just to be
here," she said.

The sun changed to a deep red, shimmering across
the green waters. Gentle swells lifted them up and down
as they continued to drift farther and farther out.

It was not yet twilight, and Tao could still see the
long line of purple hills far off in the distance. With a

nagging feeling of doubt he sat down beside Deha and Ram, wondering when they would ever see land again.

He watched slim-winged birds soaring high over-head, and once again he saw flying fish leap up and skim over the waves. He looked down into the water and saw the dark gray shadows of fish larger than himself, circling around the raft.

He sat quietly, listening to the lap of the waves.

"I smell something different," said Deha.

Tao sniffed and shook his head. "Like what?"

"A sour smell," said Deha, "in the air, like bad fish."

Tao stood up and looked around. Not far off, he saw large flocks of sea gulls and terns swooping and diving, flying about in circles. Then a high plume of spray rose out of the water, and Tao heard a soft *whoooosh* or blowing sound. A moment later another fountain of spray rose up on the other side of the raft. Tao's body stiffened as he saw another and another; white misty clouds blowing up all around them. His heart beat fast, and he remembered the drawing on the pelt. He stared against the glare of the sun just as a great flat tail rose up then slid down into the water. He stood there, hardly daring to believe his eyes. "They're here," he cried, "the fish as big as mountains."

"Where?" asked Deha.

"Everywhere," said Tao. "They surround us."

The whooooshing sounds grew louder now as the

beasts swam closer, spouting plumes of spray from the tops of their heads. Another huge tail curved up right beside the raft, then disappeared beneath the waves.

Tao's voice quivered. "Monsters," he said. "Maybe even demons."

Tao stood beside the girl, holding on to the center post, waiting. Deha kept Ram close on the leash.

The screaming flocks of birds flew nearer, circling around the raft. Terns dove into the water and came up with tiny fish wiggling in their bills. Sea gulls swarmed overhead, screeching and crying, fighting to gather food stirred up by the huge bodies of the giant fish.

Tao felt his knees shake as the blowing sounds came closer. Then, without warning, a huge black monster heaved up out of the water, like an island rising from the sea. It lay for a moment, floating on the swells beside the raft. Streams of water ran off its back as it blew out a loud *whoooooosh* from the hole on the top of its head. A cloud of mist filled the air, and Tao smelled the sickening odor of rancid fish.

Ram bristled, growling.

Deha held him back. "Do not anger the sea demons," she said, "or they will swallow us all."

The boy stood spellbound, unable to believe this wild scene. Here were the giant fish Graybeard had sketched on the pelt. Could they also be the evil spirits Zugor had called down upon them? He shivered, then shook his head. No, Graybeard and Kala taught him not to believe in such demons.

Whoooooosh. The great beast blew again. Its wide flat tail flipped into the air, all wet and gleaming in the late sunlight. Then in a swirl of water it sank beneath the waves.

Tao gasped. This was the biggest living thing he had ever seen.

A moment later two more came up. They surfaced right beside the raft and blew out a cloud of mist. Then a fourth, followed by another and another, heaving and blowing like great black demons until the air was filled with their rancid breaths.

Deha still clung to the center post. "I hear them," she said. "There must be many."

"More than I can count on my fingers," said Tao. He looked about in wonder at the huge monsters wallowing all around them. "They are like the herds on the plains," he said, "some big, some small, and some with young ones by their sides."

He stood in the middle of the raft with his legs spread apart to keep his balance as he watched the massive beasts circle closer, rolling over on their backs, blowing, and slapping the water with their tails.

Just then one of the monsters burst into the air right in front of the raft. Like a leaping salmon it flung itself completely out of the water. Its enormous body glistened in the late-afternoon sun. Tao saw the huge mouth and long armlike flippers, and the white throat and belly with many grooves. Then, with a thunderous boom, it fell back into the water, sending up showers of mist and spray.

The rush of waves crashed over the raft, pitching it up and down, rocking it violently. Tao hunched down beside Deha and Ram and held tightly to the center post. He watched as the gigantic creatures continued to leap and roll, churning the waters into billows of foam.

Soaked by the constant spray, Tao wiped his eyes. "They lift their heads out of the water and turn around slowly," he said, "as if playing with us the way a wolf cub plays with a vole."

Deha tried to laugh, but there was an edge of fear in her voice.

Now more birds came, flying out from shore to gather in swirling, screaming flocks around the wallowing beasts.

Tao stood, intrigued by this teeming display of life. If only Deha could see it, he thought, she would remember it and draw it on her sketch stones.

He was thinking of this when the thud came. It came without warning, a smashing upward thrust, as one of the monsters heaved up directly beneath them. It carried the raft on its back for a moment, lifting it high out of the water.

Deha fell across Ram and groped desperately for the center post.

Tao saw his spear rolling away. He reached out for it, lost his grip on the post, and slid down across the wet logs. He hit the water with a splash and sank into the green depths, holding his breath. He opened his eyes and saw enormous black shadows swimming all around him. He hung for a moment, looking around to get his bearings. Then he kicked and clawed, trying to reach the surface. He had almost made it when one of the monsters swam beneath him. The rush and flow of its passing sent him tumbling end over end.

Moments later, with his lungs bursting, Tao righted himself and started up again. He reached the surface, spitting water and gasping for breath. He looked around, only to see the raft drifting slowly away.

All around him he heard the loud whooooshing sounds as the massive creatures exhaled and rolled in the darkening waters. He waited to catch his breath, then struck out for the raft.

Once or twice he saw it rise up on the swells. Yet each time it seemed to be drifting farther away. Then, over the sounds of the waves, he heard Deha's voice. "Tao, where are you? Can you hear me?"

He tried to call back, but his voice was weak and drowned out by the screaming sea gulls. Once again he started out in the direction of the raft. Mist and spray lashed his eyes, blurring his vision. Occasionally he made out the dark outline of the raft only to see it disappear again in a trough. He swam steadily, yet he seemed to be getting no closer. His arms grew tired. He breathed heavily and swallowed mouthfuls of water.

Sick to his stomach, he stopped to rest again. Then he saw the long dark shadow coming directly for him. It swam slowly, rising up out of the water, blowing with a loud *whoooosh*, then coming on again until it completely filled his vision. He waited, treading water, wondering which way to turn.

Closer and closer it came, like a mountain floating down on him as he waited for the huge mouth to open and engulf him. He turned around, but there was nowhere to go, no way to escape.

Quickly he took a deep breath and ducked underwater as if to hide. He opened his eyes and cringed, for here, in the green depths, the beast looked twice as large.

He kicked out, swimming underwater to stay ahead of it. Yet the great beast followed deliberately, moving ahead without effort.

Tao reached the surface, took another quick breath, then dove down again. The monster sank beside him, and Tao looked into its tiny, lidless eye, no bigger than his fist. It gaped at him, as if pondering this insignificant creature that dared to invade its domain.

Fighting against fear and his need to breathe, Tao hung in the water, awed by the ugly beauty of the giant beast. He saw the knobby snout, the strange grooves and mottled pattern of its white throat and underbelly. Most of all, he wondered at the supple grace as it moved slowly through the water.

Then the great mouth opened and Tao felt the strong surge as he was pulled forward. Yet he saw no teeth, only long black bristles hanging down from the gaping maw. He fought desperately against the current drawing him in, when suddenly the mouth closed and he was pushed aside by the force of water. Then, with a light flick of its tail, the monster turned and disappeared into the fading light.

Unable to hold his breath any longer, Tao kicked out and swam to the surface, reaching for air. He breathed deeply and looked around, but did not see the raft. He knew he would have to find it soon, for his arms and legs felt numb from the cold and would barely move. He listened for Deha's call, but heard only the occasional sighs of the blowing monsters and the shrill cries of the birds.

The red sun dipped below the horizon, and a pinkish glow of twilight settled over the waters. Each time he lifted on a swell, Tao glanced around frantically, searching for the raft. But the wind had come up and the driving mist almost completely blinded him. Once he thought he saw the raft, and he called out. Yet even as he did, he knew that without sight, the girl could do little to help him.

With all sense of direction gone, he tried to swim again, painfully moving his tired arms, hoping he was heading in the right direction. After a few strokes he found he could not go on. His arms and legs would no longer obey. Cold and numb, he felt himself begin to sink. He kicked feebly, barely keeping his head above water. Again and again he tried to call out. Instead he swallowed mouthfuls of salt water.

Then, in the gathering darkness, he heard something new splashing through the water. He shook his head to clear his vision and saw it coming directly toward him. He turned and forced his tired arms to move as he swam to get out of its way.

He had gone only a short distance when it caught up to him and brushed against his shoulder. Tao looked down and blinked his eyes. It was Ram, with the grass rope tied around his neck and trailing loosely behind him.

Tao put his arm around the wolf dog. He reached for the rope and pulled it taut, and he knew it was attached to the raft. Deha and Ram had found a way to help him.

With his last bit of strength, Tao pulled himself along, Ram swimming close beside him. He heard Deha call, "Tao, I'm over here. Just follow the rope."

Tao wanted to rest, but he forced himself to go on. Soon he reached out and touched the heaving logs. He felt Deha's hands under his arms, pulling him up over the edge, rolling him onto the raft, where he lay gasping for breath. He put his hand out and patted Ram on the shoulder, and then smiled, glancing up at Deha. "It's a good thing you are here after all," he said.

Deha laughed. "You are safe now. That is all that matters."

The great fish and the screaming gulls were gone now. For a long time, Tao lay there resting, wondering how he and Deha would ever get back home.

14

A yellow moon trailed a rippling path across the waters as the raft continued to heave and fall with a steady rocking motion. Tao sat up, leaning against the center post, trying to stay awake. In spite of his efforts his head slumped forward on his chest and he dozed off, waking occasionally to hear the soft lapping of the waves.

He had not been sleeping long when he was awakened by Deha nudging him on the shoulder. He looked up and rubbed the sleep from his eyes.

"I hear strange things," she said, "like whispers all around us."

Tao pulled himself to his feet and looked around. The moon was directly overhead now, yet he could barely make out the land, a low dark line on the distant horizon lit by moonlight. Worst of all, they seemed to be drifting farther and farther away.

Then he, too, heard the strange whispering sounds. They were faint yet came from all around. At first he could see nothing but the patches of lacy foam on the tops of the breaking waves. Yet the noise grew more persistent and closer, a steady *splash-slap, splash-slap,* followed by a series of low hissing sounds. He squinted out across the water until his eyes became adjusted to the pale sheen of light.

Then he saw them, giant turtles, far bigger than the biggest river turtles he had ever seen. They swam by slowly, ponderously, each one as black as night.

"Turtles," he told Deha, "almost as big as the raft. They plow through the waves, leaving bright trails of foam behind them. Their heads, bigger than a man's, they lift out of the water to breathe, blowing out bubbles of froth and foam from their nostrils.

"It is wondrous. They swim strongly with big paddle-shaped flippers. There are many. They shine in the moonlight like black wet boulders. Where they all come from, I do not know."

"I hear them puffing and whispering all around us," said Deha.

Tao watched for a while as they came in twos and threes, paddling and wallowing in the swells, and he noticed they were all heading in the same direction, all swimming straight and deliberately toward land.

Then he remembered the river turtles back home in

the valley. How often he had seen them come out on land to lay their eggs in the sand. And now he was sure these big turtles were doing the same.

As he stood there heavy-eyed and tired, his gaze fell on the grass rope lying at his feet. He saw one end still tied around the peg at the front of the raft, with the other end coiled up on the wet logs. He picked it up, running his fingers over the tightly braided strands. With trembling hands he tied the free end into a big loop. Then he knelt down and leaned over the edge of the raft, holding the loop out over the water.

Soon one of the big turtles came close. He threw the rope, tossing the loop over its head. The turtle rolled and thrashed about. It caught the loop under its flipper and threw it off. Tao groaned. He pulled in the rope and made the loop smaller but not tight enough to choke.

Once again he knelt down and leaned over the water, waiting. Two more turtles swam by. They were of medium size so he let them go. He wanted the biggest one he could find.

He did not have long to wait. A few moments later, a huge one paddled up beside the raft. As it lifted its head to breathe, Tao dropped the loop, catching the turtle around the neck.

Tao stood up and spread out his legs to brace himself as the wet rope ran through his fingers. As soon as it grew taut, he let it go. The turtle plunged into the waves. With powerful strokes of its big flippers, it swam, dragging the raft behind it, determined not to be stopped.

Deha felt the motion. "We're moving," she cried. "In what direction?"

"Toward land," said Tao, "if the rope holds and the turtle does not turn around."

Slowly but steadily the raft plowed through the rough seas, pitching and bobbing as it plunged ahead.

Still weak and light-headed from his ordeal with the giant fish, there was little more Tao could do now. He sat down next to Deha, where he could hold on to the center post.

Ram sat beside them, his front legs spread out for balance.

They sailed along slowly, smashing through the waves, sliding up and down the swells. Each time they rose up on a swell, Tao could make out the dark hills of land on the horizon. They could only hang on and wait as clouds of mist and soaking spray washed over them.

Drowsy and sick, Tao fought against the urge to sleep. He shook his head and tried to keep his eyes open. Yet he dozed off as the raft rocked and lurched over the heavy swells.

Tao awakened to the crash of waves against the shore.

Little by little it grew louder, and he knew they were getting close to land.

Half asleep, he started to get up. He was almost on his feet, when the raft jolted as if hit by something from below. It tilted sharply, throwing Deha and Ram and all their belongings into the crashing waves.

Tao flew over the side. At the same time he saw the rope snap. He reached out and grabbed it, then felt the strong tug as the big turtle dragged him through the water. But he could not hang on. His arms were still heavy and he let the rope go.

He kicked feebly, trying to keep his head above water. He saw Ram bobbing in the waves, far off to one side. He opened his mouth and tried to shout but swallowed a mouthful of salt water. Then he saw the wolf dog disappear into the surf.

He looked around for Deha, wondering how she would find her way without someone to guide her. He tried to call, but it was no use; his faint words were smothered by the crashing surf.

He kicked and squirmed to stay afloat. Yet time after time he sank below the waves, only to come up spitting and gasping for breath. Weary and tired from the long strain, he could go on no longer.

His last thoughts were of Deha and Ram. Nothing else mattered, not even the antelope pelt with the map still tucked under his belt. He felt his tired body go limp, and he sank down into darkness. The waves pushed him along, and moments later the surf washed him up onto the beach, where he lay wet and unmoving. Only the turtles saw him as they crawled up the sandy beach to lay their eggs.

15

Tao opened his eyes in the dim light. He blinked and sat up, pushing the soft skin robe from his shoulders. He looked around and saw that he was in a small cave. Deha sat nearby with her back propped against the wall. Ram lay close beside her, his head on his paws.

Deha heard the boy move. "Are you awake?"

"Yes," said Tao. "Where are we?"

"I don't know," said Deha. "I only remember being carried here."

"By who?"

Deha shrugged. "A man, a strange man. I heard him speak, but I was sick from swallowing water and half asleep and did not understand all that he said."

Tao got to his feet. He reached out to steady himself, then glanced around in surprise. Crude markings of fish, star creatures, pelicans, and other birds covered the walls on both sides of the small cavern. He even saw an unfinished sketch of the head with many arms and the strange animals without legs. He walked slowly around the cave, studying the scribbles and scrawls, wondering who had made them. Then more surprises awaited him. On the floor, in the center of the cavern, lay all their belongings: the skin sacks, the grass rope, his spear, even Deha's flute. His skin pouch lay beside them. He opened it and found his shining stone, his slates, his leather thongs, and firestones. He reached down and felt the antelope pelt and his flint knife still tucked safely under his belt.

On the hearthstone, near the entrance, the embers of a small fire still burned, and beside it lay a strange, freshly caught fish, as flat and as round as an acorn cake. Beside it lay some turtle eggs and four large crabs.

Tao shook his head in wonder. "Who is this man who looks after us?" he asked.

"He is strong," said Deha, "very strong. He picked me up off the beach with one hand, and I felt him throw you over his other shoulder and carry us here."

Tao walked around the room again, deep in thought. He picked up the robe from the floor and rubbed the palm of his hand over the soft white fur. "This is not ibex or mouflon," he said. "It is not roe deer or bison. It is different." He pointed to the food lying by the fire. "And this fish I have never seen before. Everything is strange. Yet it is left here for us."

Tao found a pile of sticks and kindling on the floor

near the side of the cave. He put some on the smouldering embers, and the fire leaped into bright yellow flames.

Deha cut the fish, and they roasted the strips over the fire on the end of Tao's flint knife. They cracked open the crab claws using two stones and picked out the meat. Along with the turtle eggs it made a tasty meal, and they shared it all with Ram.

After they ate Tao stood at the entrance and looked out at the water and the wide beach where the turtles had come in. Far off in the other direction he could make out the low cliffs and the piles of rock jutting out into the water. He stood there for a long time, looking around. Then he said, "I do not know where we are or who brought us here, but the children back home wait for us and we must find the medicine."

Deha called Ram and tied the leash to his collar. "I will go with you," she said.

Tao spread out the antelope pelt on the floor. Once again he ran his finger along the margins. "This is what we must find," he said. "The ribbonlike leaves and tiny flowers growing on shells."

Ram led Deha on the leash as they made their way down a steep path to the water. There they turned away from the rocks and up along the wide beach. Tao saw the deep furrows in the sand where the turtles had crawled up the beach the night before.

They walked slowly as Tao searched along the water's edge. He stepped over windrows of empty shells, while many crablike creatures darted across the wet sand in front of them. He found flat, crusty star creatures with five arms, and many spiny objects that looked like chestnut burrs.

Clumps of green and brown weeds covered the beach, with more empty shells and an occasional dead fish scattered among them.

Tao shook his head. "There are many brown spongy things," he told Deha, "but no long ribbon-shaped leaves or flowers."

Deha stopped and pushed her dark hair over her shoulders. "Would not the plants grow away from the water, somewhere far up on the beach?" she said. "And maybe the flowers, too?"

Together they walked up to the sand dunes. There Tao found many empty shells, some like fans, others coiled like snail shells, and still others like the mussel shells found in the lakes back home. But all of them were bleached and dried out by the sun. None had flowers growing on them. They searched most of the morning but found only strings of purple blossoms on the sand vines and some tiny daisies growing among the clumps of beach grass.

Empty-handed, they turned and went back to the beach. Tao let Ram off the leash so he could run free, then took Deha by the hand and led her down to where the shoreline became a rocky coast. Giant columns of stone rose high out of the sand. Cautiously Tao led Deha between them while flocks of tiny sand birds scooted in and out, racing with the surf.

Here they found the raft washed up on the beach, half buried in the sand. Tao started to brush it off, then changed his mind. "The raft is still good," he said. "So first let us find the medicine."

Far out beyond the waves great fish leaped into the air, with clouds of birds swarming around them. Wherever he looked, Tao saw living things flying and swimming, creeping and crawling.

He was watching all this when he saw Ram playing with something on the beach. It was a long flat object with a whiplike stem. The wolf dog shook it in his jaws and dragged it across the sand.

Tao walked closer, still holding Deha by the hand. Then he stopped in surprise. He saw that it was a long ribbonlike leaf, dark brown, smooth, and shiny. A weed from the Great Waters. He picked it up and held one end high over his head, letting the other end hang down in long folds around his feet.

He held it out to Deha. She reached for it and felt the long leathery folds. "Yes," she said. "Like the leaf you saw on the antelope pelt. This surely is the medicine."

Tao rolled it up and stuffed it into his skin sack. They

walked farther down the beach, looking for more. Not far away they found another. Tao reached down to pick it up, when suddenly he saw a man step from behind one of the big rocks. He was not tall, but he was powerfully built with great brawny arms and heavy shoulders covered with hair. Thick dark eyebrows gave him a haunting scowl.

Tao fell back, pushing Deha behind him. He gripped his spear and held it ready.

Deha felt the sudden tension. "What is it?" she asked.

"A Neander," whispered Tao.

Deha's hand trembled. "Like Zugor?"

"I don't know," said Tao. "Younger, stronger."

The Neander stood there, slightly hunched over. He had a flat nose that covered most of his face, and a square protruding jaw. He stared at them, watching them closely. He held a large stone in the palm of his right hand, hefting it, as if ready to throw. With his other hand he gripped a leather thong tied to a large plump animal slung over his shoulder. He gave a rough grunt and stepped forward.

Tao moved back again, almost stumbling over Deha. He smiled to show a sign of friendship, but still held his spear out in front of him.

Ram walked up to the man, wagging his tail.

Deha pressed close to Tao. "Maybe this is the man who saved us."

"He looks strong enough," said Tao. "He carries

no weapon except a stone, and Ram seems to know him."

The man wore only a soft animal skin tied about his waist. He stepped closer, and his face wrinkled up in a twisted grin, showing a row of strong teeth. He dropped the stone and held up his hand in a sign of peace.

Tao waited a moment, then pointed inland to the mountains, barely visible in the far distance. "You understand talk of clan people?" he asked.

The Neander stopped where he was. "Little," he said.

Tao pointed at Deha and himself. "Are you the one who saved us?"

The man nodded. "You come from sea, bellyful of water, not good."

"We wish to thank you for helping us," said Deha.

The man stood there, grinning like a child but saying nothing.

"What name do they call you?" asked Tao.

"Shag, like bird that live by sea." The man lowered the animal he was carrying to the ground and threw back his shoulders to rest.

Tao glanced down at it. His eyes widened and he turned to Deha. "It is the animal without legs."

"Seal," said the man. "Good food." He patted the skin he was wearing. "Make good robe."

Tao leaned down and ran his hand over the animal's

fur. He tried to lift it but it was as heavy as a full-grown man.

Shag grunted. "I carry," he said. He reached down, picked up the seal, and threw it over his back. Then he turned and called over his shoulder, "Teal, come."

A moment later, like magic, three more Neanders appeared from behind the stones. One was a woman; the other two were a girl and a little boy. They looked up at Tao and Deha with dark, wide eyes.

"Is Shag family," said the man with pride. "Is Teal, is Grebe, is little Auk." He stood for a moment, still grinning. Then he looked down at the long brown leaf lying at Tao's feet. "You look kelp?" he asked.

"Kelp?" said Tao as he reached down and picked up the long brown ribbon. "Yes, we look for kelp."

"Many summers past, another man come look for kelp," said Shag. "He bring home to clan." Shag pointed to the boy and girl. "Tomorrow children help you find." He shifted the heavy seal to his other shoulder. "Now we go have food."

Tao took Deha's hand as they followed the man up the steep path to the cave. There Deha helped Teal skin the seal and cut the meat into strips. They roasted it, then sat on the floor around the hearty feast.

Before they ate, Shag raised his arms to the ceiling of the little cave, saying, "We thank Spirit of Great Waters for good food, for us and our children."

Tao gave Ram some of the blubber, some turtle eggs, and strips of red meat.

"Wolf is good," said Shag, "good for clan people who hunt."

"You do not hunt?" asked Tao.

The man shook his head. "Little," he said. "Mostly fish."

"Do you see many clan people?" Deha asked.

"Only clan people from lake come," said Shag. "Chase us away, sometimes kill Neanders. They take fish, turtle eggs, shells, seals, everything. We hide till gone."

"But this is your land, too," said Deha.

The man shrugged. "Clan people too many. We not many. Not fight."

Deha sighed. "It is strange," she said. "Here there is enough for all."

Shag looked at them. "Why you come?"

"To find medicine," said Tao.

"Kelp medicine?"

"That and more," said Tao.

"What for, medicine?"

"For sick children," said Tao. He took the antelope pelt from his belt and unrolled it, holding it up for Shag to see. He pointed to the flowers growing on the shells. "This morning we found the long leaves. Now we must find the flowers."

Shag looked at the pelt, studying it for a long time. Then his eyes narrowed in thought as he remembered.

"Ah," he said, "I know picture. Man who came for kelp make it."

Tao looked up, startled. "It was Graybeard?"

"Yes, name Graybeard. He come many times. Good to Neanders." He pointed at the pelt. "I watch him make pictures with burning stick." He patted the floor of the cave beside him. "Right here in cave."

Tao leaned forward eagerly. "If you saw Graybeard make this picture, then you must know where the medicine is."

"Yes," said Shag, "I help Graybeard find. But medicine not flowers."

Tao looked down at the pelt once again and shook his head. "Not shells with flowers on them?"

"No, not flowers," said Shag. "Tomorrow I show you."

Shag stood up, and once again Tao noticed the heavy shoulders, the strong back muscles. "You friend of Graybeard," said Shag. "Now I show you something else." He took a pine stick and rubbed it in seal fat to make a torch. Then he turned to Tao. "Come."

Deha and Ram stayed behind with the family while Tao followed the man through a narrow tunnel at the back of the cave. They felt their way around a sharp curve and twice they crawled on their hands and knees before reaching a small cavern. There Shag lit more torches and wedged them into cracks in the wall.

Tao looked up, then stepped back in surprise. There,

on the far wall, was a large painting of an animal without legs. "A seal?" he said.

"No," said Shag, "is sea lion—bigger than seal."

Tao stared at it, admiring the smooth blend of colors, the massive shape of the neck and shoulders, even the unerring style. It had the master's touch.

"Graybeard do this for us," said Shag. "Now we have own paintings."

Tao looked around at the other walls, where many of the drawings were merely crude pictures scratched into the stone. One showed a great fish spitting water from its head.

Shag smiled. "I try draw, but not good."

Tao saw paintings of seals and odd-looking seabirds. He pointed to an unfinished sketch of a head with many arms.

"Is devilfish," said Shag. "Good food."

The boy glanced around the room, admiring Graybeard's painting of the sea lion and the meaningful but clumsy efforts of the Neanders to imitate him. He told Shag how the old man had taught him to draw and paint.

Shag nodded expectantly. "You paint for us," he said. "Bring luck for hunting and fishing." He waved his hand around the little cavern. "Is room for many more. I tell other Neanders come see."

Tao agreed. "But first I must find the medicine."

"Tomorrow," said Shag. "Tomorrow I show where is medicine."

They started back through the little tunnel and had almost reached the cave when Tao heard the lilting notes of the flute. He smiled. Deha was playing for Teal and the children.

16

■■■ They walked down the path to the beach, then turned up to where the rocks extended into the water. The sun was already high, warming the sand as Shag led them over the jumble of rocks. Tao and the two children followed close behind. Teal took Deha and Ram along an easier path just below the cliffs.

Clouds of sea gulls swooped and dove over their heads. Shag stopped near the edge of the surf, where it splashed and flowed over the stones. Here, many deep pools of water filled the depressions between the rocks. Patches of kelp grew in each pool like miniature meadows, rising and falling as the surf rolled in and out.

Shag waved his hand, indicating the scattered pools that were strung out along the rocky coast as far as they could see. He held up two fingers. "Sea come in two times day. When go out leave water in pool between rocks."

Tao looked down into one of the little ponds, amazed

at the many colorful creatures living within its shallow depths.

He watched bright orange-and-red star animals crawl across the sandy bottom amid the waving fronds of kelp. Round spiny creatures like tiny hedgehogs moved slowly between stands of gaudy yellow fingers, while reddish-brown crabs scurried along on stilted legs. Brightly frilled worms squirmed and swayed between clusters of blue-black mussels.

Then he saw a devilfish, the head with many arms. It flowed across the sandy bottom, stalking one of the crabs. He watched, fascinated, as the arms reached out quickly and caught the crab then hauled it off into a crevasse in the rocks.

Tao turned his attention to the waving fronds of kelp. He lay on his belly and reached down to pull one up. He yanked and tugged but found the roots firmly anchored to the rocks.

Shag laughed and called the children. "Grebe, Auk, come, pick kelp."

Giggling and pushing, the children jumped into the pool, wincing as they stepped on the sharp barnacles and other shells growing beneath their feet. They waded up to their waists, reaching down to grab the rubbery plants by the long stems. With a sharp twist they wrenched them free and handed them to Tao.

Tao grinned as he carried them high up the beach. There he spread them out on the flat stones to dry in the sun. The children continued to pull up the long strands of kelp, while Tao trudged back and forth with the rubbery plants draped over his arms and shoulders.

When he had enough, Tao turned to Shag. "Now I must find the other medicine," he said.

Shag walked to one of the larger pools and pointed. "Medicine like flower is here."

Tao peered into the clear water, his eyes searching the pool. He saw the many mussel shells, the creeping snails, the round spiny creatures, and the colorful sea stars.

Shag stood beside him, waiting. "Look for flower," he said.

A flower growing underwater? Tao shrugged. How could that be? Once more he stared into the pool, looking around the edges and into the depths, but he saw no flowers. He moved to the other side, where the sun was at his back. Still he saw no flower. He threw up his hands.

Shag laughed. "Grebe find flower."

The girl lay on her stomach and plunged her arm into the water. Tao looked to where she pointed. Then he too saw it, the delicate beauty of a small golden flower about the size of his little finger. He blinked and looked again. It grew on a stem like a mushroom, with petals of long yellow tentacles waving gently in the water. He continued to stare, and his eyes picked out another and another and yet another, each one growing on a large reddish-brown shell.

Little Auk stepped into the pool, and Tao watched as the boy reached down with his flint knife to pry up one of the red shells. As soon as the boy's hand came close to the shell, the yellow flower mysteriously disappeared, drawing within itself.

The boy went on to pry around the edges of the shell, carefully working it loose from the rock. He lifted it up and handed it to Tao. It was rough and knobby on the outside and as large as Tao's two hands cupped together.

The little flowerlike creature was now nothing but a flabby nubbin of flesh clinging to the outside of the shell. Shag touched it with the end of his finger. "See, no flower," he said, "only look same."

Using his flint knife, Tao scraped out the layer of pink-and-white meat, which he knew now was the medicine he needed, leaving a lining of gleaming silver on the inside of the beautiful abalone shell.

Now, with the help of Grebe and Auk, Tao pried off more of the large shells. He scooped out the meat and carried it up to the beach, where he laid it out in the bright sunlight. Dried, it would be lighter. This way Tao and Deha could carry much more back to the clan.

Teal watched as Tao spread the meat out on the stones. She smiled. "Not for birds?"

Tao glanced up at the many seabirds flying all around.

"No," he said, "not for birds. For me." He went on digging out more and more of the big shells. He worked hard, scooping out the meat, carrying it up to the stones high on the beach, making trip after trip.

He had just gone down to the pools for another handful when he heard Teal call after him, "Birds come, Tao. Birds come."

Tao spun around. He heard the screeching, whining cries, and he looked back to see swarms of seabirds diving low over the beach. As he walked toward them he realized they were flocks of terns and gulls, swooping down, stealing his shellfish. He wrapped his bad leg around his spear and vaulted up the beach.

Trembling with rage, he waded into the wheeling mass of birds, swinging his spear and shouting to drive them off. They easily dodged his blows, then swooped down behind his back to steal another scrap of meat. He yelled, threw stones and fistfuls of sand in a futile effort to chase them away.

Ram rushed in to help, leaping and nipping at the birds' tails. But it was like chasing the wind. No sooner had they scared off one flock than another appeared seemingly out of nowhere.

Grebe and little Auk joined in the game. They ran from one side to the other, laughing and giggling, waving their arms, throwing empty shells and clumps of weeds at the wheeling mass of birds. But it did little good, as the gulls and terns kept coming back to pick up the remaining scraps of meat.

In the midst of it all, Tao turned to see Shag holding his sides, roaring with laughter as he stood and watched.

When it was over, the only things left were the long brown ribbons of kelp lying in the sun. The shell meat was gone. Tao tried to catch his breath. He looked around at the children, still jumping and giggling with delight. Slowly his anger faded, and he too began to laugh. He picked up his spear and shook his fist at the retreating gulls.

"They will get no more," he told Shag. "If I cannot dry the medicine here, I will carry it home as it is, even though it be wet and heavy."

Shag walked over to him, still chuckling. He pointed toward the water. "Plenty more," he said. "We help."

Shag, Teal, and the two children all took turns gathering the big shells and cutting out the meat. Deha wrapped it in bundles of kelp, and Teal stuffed them into sealskin sacks that she had made for them. She filled two heavy sacks for Tao and two light ones for Deha, which would be as much as they could carry.

"Now you have medicine," said Shag. "Tomorrow you go back to clan." Then he smiled. "Tonight you paint for us."

Toward evening more Neanders came to Shag's cavern. Silently, as if out of nowhere, they trudged up the steep path to the little cave in small groups: men, women, and children, seven families in all.

Deha, Teal, and the other women prepared a supper with the sea trout, mackerel, and rock crabs that the men had brought. They sat cross-legged on the floor and enjoyed their meal, and sipped birch tea from large clamshells.

When supper was over, Shag stood up and motioned to the seven men and the two older boys. "Come," he said. "Now Tao will paint for us."

Carrying torches made from pine knots and seal fat, the men followed Shag and Tao through the winding tunnel and into the little cavern. There they sat in a circle, quietly waiting for the artist to begin.

Tao stood in front of a wide area of untouched wall, wondering what to draw. He wanted to do something these fishermen would know, something they might see every day. He thought of seals, of devilfish and sea lions, but he was not that familiar with the animals of the sea and hesitated to try something he did not know.

To give himself time to think, he knelt down on the floor beside a row of large clamshells filled with black, orange, and red paints that Shag had provided. He spent time examining the long willow-stick brushes tipped with boar's hair. His mind raced ahead as he aimlessly inspected each brush, each piece of chalk, at the same time trying desperately to think of something these men would prize.

The moments passed, and he began to sense the dead silence of his audience, questioning, waiting. With a shrug of his shoulders he got to his feet. He would do the thing he knew best, a bison.

Then he stopped and thought, and smiled to himself. Only a few days ago he had been swimming in the waters with the great fish. He had been close enough to reach out and touch them. They had stared at him with their tiny eyes, and he had looked into their gaping mouths. What beast would he know better?

With his charcoal he drew a sweeping, crescent-shaped line across the wall. An arm's length below that he drew an inverted bow, curving it up to connect both ends of the first crescent. Toward one end he marked off a small dorsal fin, and beyond that a great forked tail. Next he drew the gaping mouth, and just behind it a small eye. Finally he sketched in the long front flippers.

The Neanders stood up now, nodding and murmuring their approval.

"It is great fish we call whale," said Shag.

"Ah," said Tao, "whale, yes." He went on with his work. He took one of the brushes, dipped it into the black paint, and brushed it over the back from head to tail. With a chunk of white chalk he filled in the sides and belly, then drew in the furrowed lines under the throat.

He stepped back for a moment to study his work.

Shag stood beside him, a big grin on his rugged face. "Is finished?" he asked.

Tao shook his head and asked, "Do you have eggs?"

Shag's eyes widened. "What kind, what for eggs?"

"Goose eggs, swan eggs, any kind," said Tao. "Then I will show you."

Shag nodded and sent one of the boys back through the cave. A short while later the boy returned with four duck eggs. Tao broke each one and separated the yolks from the whites. The whites he placed in a large abalone shell. With a clean brush he washed the egg white lightly over the painting. Instantly the picture glowed, wet and shiny like a living whale leaping from the sea.

"Ahaaaaaaaa." A low sound of approval swept through the little cavern as the Neanders gathered around the painting, staring and pointing with excitement.

Shag put his hand on the boy's shoulder. "Like Graybeard, you good friend of Neanders."

Tao felt a glow of pride as he made his way back through the tunnel with the others.

This time he did not hear Deha playing her flute. Instead he found her standing near the entrance to the cave. There, with a flint chisel and a hammer stone, she etched out a picture for the children, who described the many arms, the slitted eyes, and the elusive beauty of a devilfish.

Tao stepped back in surprise, admiring the sweeping flow of the etching. It was truly a devilfish, yet he knew she had never seen one before.

The Neanders gathered around her in silent wonder, watching her work.

Shag turned to Tao. "You come soon again," he said. "Then Deha paint in cave too."

Deha smiled at the Neander's words.

The next morning Tao went down to the raft. It was stranded high on the beach. He brushed off the sand with the branch of a bayberry bush and scooped around the edges with a large shell.

Grabbing the logs at the front end, Tao tried to pull it down into the water. He heaved and tugged, but the heavy raft never budged.

Grebe and Auk came down to help. They pushed while Tao pulled. They grunted and groaned. Still it would not move.

Tao walked around the raft, trying to think of some way to get it into the water.

Just then Shag came down to the beach. He looked out at the sea. "Tide come in soon," he said. "You go now river take you fast up."

Tao knew what Shag meant. If they left now they could catch the incoming current flowing upstream. If not they would have to wait another day. "We will go now," he said, "if I can find a way to get the raft into the water."

Shag walked around the stranded raft, studying it for a moment. Then he said, "I fix." He reached down and lifted the front end of the raft with his big hands. His powerful arms bulged, and the muscles on his back rippled.

Tao's mouth dropped open as he watched the brawny Neander drag the heavy raft down to the water's edge. There he dropped it and looked up with a big grin. "Now can go," he said.

Tao left Deha and the children to load the raft with the medicine sacks and their belongings, while he went up behind the sand dunes to cut two long birch poles.

It was still early when the Neander families came to the beach to see them off.

Deha and Ram climbed aboard the raft as Tao thanked Shag and his family for all their help. Then he poled the raft out beyond the surf.

Shag called after them, "You come soon back."

Deha waved. "We will," she shouted, "we will."

17

They caught the incoming current, and the strong tidewaters swept them through the cove and far up into the mouth of the river. Deha helped, pushing hard with her long pole, and Tao guided the raft between the winding meadows of tall reeds. Tao knew that most of their journey would have to be on foot but he planned to go upstream as far as the current would take them.

The afternoon sun beat down on the marshlands, and the shell meat in the skin sacks warmed up, giving off a strong fishy odor. Flocks of screeching gulls swooped and circled around the raft. These in turn attracted terns, cormorants, and pelicans, until great clouds of screaming birds swirled overhead. Some of the more brazen gulls landed on the raft to peck at the skin sacks, keeping Ram busy chasing them off.

By the middle of the afternoon they were well beyond the reeds and into the shoals and sandbars. Here schools of salmon still thrashed and jumped on their way upstream to their breeding grounds, while shaggy brown bears splashed through the water, scooping out the fish or catching them in their jaws. Many of the bears stood up in the water, sniffing as they saw the raft go by. Tao kept well out in midstream, for he knew the bears might be tempted by the odor of the smelly shellfish.

Soon Tao felt the current beginning to turn, and it became harder and harder to push ahead.

Tao was poling the raft between two long sandbars when he noticed a big she-bear staring at him. At first he thought she smelled the shellfish, and he pushed hard to move farther away. Then he saw two cubs on a sandbar on the opposite side of the raft. The she-bear dropped down on all fours and came charging across the water, and Tao knew the cubs were hers.

Deha heard the loud splash. "What is it?" she asked.

"A big she-bear," yelled Tao. "We're in between her and her cubs. She's coming after us." Quickly he reached into his leather pouch for his shining stone. It was mixed up with his flints, his slates, and chalks. He groped around, rummaging through the bag, but could not find it.

Ram stood growling and Deha braced herself against the center post as the angry bear came charging through the water. The old she-bear roared in fury, beating up a shower of spray as she lunged at the raft.

At the last moment, Tao pulled out the shining stone, but now the bear was too close. She reached out and clawed at the logs, tipping the raft at a sharp angle. Tao tried to push her off with the pole. With an angry growl she grabbed it in her jaws and snapped it in half.

The raft tipped higher and things began to slide as the old bear heaved herself up, trying to climb aboard. Tao whacked her with the broken pole. Once again she grabbed it in her jaws. This time she pulled it out of his hands and tossed it into the water.

Quickly he glanced around, looking for something to throw. Without stopping to think he grabbed a sack of the shellfish meat and flung it in her face.

Startled by the blow, she let go of the raft and backed away, clutching the sack of meat in her arms. She stood in water up to her waist, floundering about as if trying to decide what to do next. By this time Tao had the shining stone in his hand. He caught the sunlight and flashed it in her eyes. She shook her head and blinked. With an angry snort she shied away, then waded past the raft to join her cubs on the sandbar.

Without waiting Tao picked up Deha's pole and pushed the raft farther upstream. He glanced back to see the two cubs fighting over the sack of shellfish meat. Only then did he realize he had thrown away one of his precious bags of medicine.

Annoyed with himself, Tao pushed hard to drive the raft on up the river. He glided under overhanging branches of swamp willows and steered around snags of rocks and sunken logs jutting up out of the water.

Deha helped, poling with the spear. But the current had almost completely turned now, and it became increasingly difficult to fight against it.

Tao jumped into the shallow water and pushed the raft ahead of him. But he soon heard the roaring sound of the cataracts, and he knew they could go no farther. The rest of the journey would have to be on foot.

They rested awhile on the bank, then Tao tied the three remaining sacks of shell meat together and threw them over his shoulder. The heavy weight bent him over, but he wrapped his bad leg around his spear and started inland. Ram led Deha on the leash, and Tao followed, slipping and sliding on the steep slopes and picking his way through the deep ravines.

The gulls and terns had long since disappeared, but now a pair of ravens followed them, cawing harshly in their ears as they made their way through the dark forest. The pesky birds flew from tree to tree just above their heads. Tao knew they were in no danger, but he was afraid other beasts might be attracted by the raucous calls.

They stopped for the night in the middle of a pine forest, where Tao was glad to put down the heavy sacks. He started a fire, and Deha roasted some mushrooms and chunks of flatfish they had brought with them from the Great Waters. After that Tao piled up beds of pine boughs. Then, tired from the long journey, they tried to get some sleep.

They had barely settled down when they were awakened by the rustling of a prowling animal. Tao jumped up and reached for his spear. He glanced about quickly. Satisfied that their belongings and the three sacks of medicine were safe beside Deha, he walked around slowly, peering into the darkness with Ram crouching by his side.

At first he saw only the wavering shadows of the low-growing laurel bushes. Then, just outside the ring of firelight, he saw many pairs of eyes glowing eerily in the night. He heard a chorus of fiendish giggles, and his body stiffened. It was a pack of hungry hyenas lurking just beyond the fire. He was sure they were attracted by the strong odor of fish, waiting only for a chance to dash in and grab whatever they could.

When they saw Tao up and moving about, they shrieked and yowled their peculiar hideous giggles.

Ram charged at them, growling and snapping to chase them off. But he was one against many. Tao rushed at them with a flaming pine torch. It drove them back, but not for long. No sooner did Tao and Ram run them off than the hyenas came back again, prowling closer than ever.

Deha sat up, her back against a large boulder, a heavy

pine club in her hand. She kept the three sacks of medicine close beside her. "How many are there?" she asked.

"Three or four," Tao lied, not wanting to frighten her. He continued to stand guard near the fire, chasing the hyenas away time after time as they became more daring.

Closer and closer they came, sneaking in from all sides. When Tao lunged at one, another came in from behind to take its place.

Panting and out of breath, Ram raced about frantically, chasing the vicious beasts from one side to the other as they taunted him and drew him out into the darkness.

All night long Tao stayed up fighting them off. He shook his head to keep awake as the gleaming eyes slinked along the edges of the firelight. He counted eight pairs, then ten, then twelve. But he knew there must be many more.

After a while he found himself nodding off even as he listened to the shrill chorus of snarls and giggles.

Then, just before daylight, a big male hyena, bolder than the others, dashed in past the fire. Tao spun around and jabbed it in the ribs with his spear. The hyena ran off and Tao went after him, chasing him far into the dim light. Ram followed, snapping at the beast's hind legs, holding it at bay as Tao tried to kill it with his spear.

In the midst of it all, Tao heard Deha's shout. "Get, get out of here!" she yelled.

Tao rushed back to help. He found Deha standing near the edge of the firelight, surrounded by the prowling beasts. She spun around, swinging her club in a fit of blind fury. She struck two across the back, sending them yelping off into the forest. But for every one she drove away, another sneaked in from behind to take its place.

Tao stood beside her, swinging and jabbing with his spear. Exhausted, they managed to drive off the rest of the stubborn beasts, but not before they had lost another sack of the precious medicine.

Deha sat down beside the boulder. "I'm sorry," she said. "There were too many. I could not stop them all."

"It's all right," said Tao, breathing hard. "Thanks to you we still have the last two sacks of medicine."

"But will that be enough?" asked Deha.

Tao tried to reassure her. "They are the two heavy sacks, and Kala will know how to make it do."

A short while later they heard the pack of scavengers off in the distance, snarling and fighting over the stolen meat.

Early morning light beamed through the pine branches as Tao picked up the heavy sacks of meat and slung them over his shoulder. Wearily he plodded along, his footsteps heavy with fatigue.

Ram led the way, guided by Tao's commands, and

Deha held on to the leash. They made their way around rocks and boulders, across streams, and up and down the many hills. Tao hunched over and forced himself to keep up as they trudged along the banks of the winding river.

Time after time, other hyenas followed as they picked up the strong odor, waiting for a chance to steal the last of the meat. Whenever he stopped to rest, Tao heard them sulking and snarling in the shadows not far behind. At night he let Deha sleep while he and Ram stood guard around a blazing fire.

On the third day, Tao staggered along in a daze, half asleep, tripping over roots, bumping into trees. He followed close behind Deha and Ram as they forced their way through thickets of bramble and scrub wood.

It was midmorning when they reached the slough. Tao heard the reed warblers singing and the harsh *kreck-kreck* of the moorhens, and he knew he was home in the Land of the Valley People. He threw himself down to rest. When Deha and Ram were ready to go on, Tao could barely get to his feet. He staggered and fell, unable to go any farther.

He lay in the shade of a clump of birch trees. There he laid the two sacks of medicine close beside him. "Go to the camp of the Valley People," he told Deha. "Ram knows the way. It is not far. Let him bring Volt or one of the hunters."

"What about the hyenas?" said Deha. "There are more around. If I take the medicine they will leave you alone."

Tao shook his head slowly and gritted his teeth. "No," he said. "You cannot see, and it is too heavy. Go with Ram. I will wait here."

Ram walked off a few steps, leading Deha. When he saw Tao still lying on the ground, he turned back, whimpering.

Tao pointed. "Go!" he ordered. "Take Deha to camp. Bring Volt."

Ram looked back once more, then started off for the distant cliffs, with Deha holding fast to the leash.

As soon as they were gone, Tao placed the spear by his side and tied the sacks to his wrist. Now if the hyenas came to steal the meat, they would be sure to wake him. Then he lay back in the soft grass and closed his eyes.

Sleep came long and deep before the dream woke him, a wild, hideous dream full of blood and violence. Hyenas crept out of the tall grass, tongues hanging out like hungry wolf dogs. They giggled and snarled and sniffed around him. He felt their fetid breath on his face and smelled the sickening odor of their bodies. He cringed and rolled aside as one big male opened its jaws just above his face, ready to strike.

Zugor came, his hair flying all around him. He picked up the spear and plunged it into the animal's side, pinning it to the ground. He laughed a wild, crazy laugh as he grabbed Tao's flint knife and cut the animal's head off.

Tao half opened his eyes. He saw the branches of the birch trees and the blue sky high above. He heard a howl of wild laughter, "Tee-tee-hee, tee-hee-hee," and a shrill voice screeching, "The magic, the magic, now I have the magic!"

The dream kept going around and around in his mind until he awoke with a start to see Volt and Deha standing over him, with Ram close beside them. He felt his heart pounding. He sat up and rubbed his eyes. "I was dreaming," he said. "I dreamt that Zugor came and saved me from the hyenas."

Volt stared down at him for a moment, then shook his head and grunted. "It was no dream, boy. Look around you."

Tao came fully awake. Painfully he climbed to his feet. A short distance away lay the body of a hyena. Next to it, the butt end of his spear was jammed into the soft earth, with the grisly head of the hyena impaled on its point.

Tao blinked his eyes in disbelief.

"The Neander from the Land of the Mountain People," said Volt. "I saw him running away as we came through the trees, laughing like a crazy fool."

"It was Zugor," said Deha. "I heard his laugh."

Tao shook his head. He glanced down at the dead animal, then up at the severed head, still dripping blood. Why would Zugor do this?

He saw his skin pouch hanging from the shaft of the spear, tied by its shoulder strap. He reached for it and opened it and thrust his hand inside. His flints were still there. Then a knot of fear tightened in the pit of his stomach. His shining stone was missing. He glanced around, but he knew, even without looking, the sacks of medicine were gone too.

18

They walked across the open plains, heading for the camp of the Valley People.

Volt led the way, all the while grumbling about Tao's foolish wanderings. "Always you go off alone to far places with only a wolf dog or a blind girl to help you. You visit strange people in other clans, where you know not what to expect. Is it any wonder you find trouble?" Volt went on muttering, half aloud.

Caught up in his own thoughts and chiding himself for his failure to bring back the medicine, Tao heard little of what his father said. Weary from his long journey, he hobbled along beside Deha, who followed Ram on the leash.

"I will go to Zugor's cave," said Tao, "and make him give back the medicine and the shining stone."

Deha shook her head. "Never," she said. "I know Zugor; he will never do it."

"Why?" asked Tao. "Of what good is the medicine

to him? He knows nothing about it. How can he use it?"

"Think," said Deha. "If you were to cure the children, or even my blindness, Zugor's demons would end. He would have nothing with which to threaten the people."

Tao nodded. "He makes fools of them," he said.

As they pushed through the waist-high grass, Tao looked up to see several vultures soaring low in the brazen sky. Many of them landed some distance away. Then another and another swooped down.

Volt stopped. He lifted his hand to shield his eyes against the sun and stared out across the plains. "Something dead way over there," he said. "Could be antelope or roe deer. Maybe Sandar left a kill."

The big man walked toward it. As Volt and the others approached the feast, the vultures hobbled off. Stern-faced and angry, the big birds gathered in a wide circle, just out of reach.

Volt reached the spot. He poked at the spoils with his spear and shook his head, baffled. "What is it?"

Tao came abreast of him. He drew in his breath as he saw the heavy sealskin bags and smelled the strong odor. "The stolen sacks of shell meat," he said.

Deha came up, sniffing the air. "The medicine?"

"Yes," said Tao as he reached down and picked up one of the sacks, which was still full. He threw it over his shoulder and shook his head in anger. "That madman Zugor had no use for it, so he left it for the vultures."

Volt shrugged and spat in the dust. "What did you expect from a Neander?" he growled.

A short while later Volt led them between the boulders near the foot of the cliffs, where they turned and made their way through the oak wood.

As they walked along the trail leading into camp, Tao saw Kala standing in the middle of the path, her hands on her hips. With an angry frown she clicked her tongue and shook her head. Then she walked up and threw her arms around him. "You are late," she said, "but you are back."

"With only some of the medicine," said Tao.

"Never mind," she said. "You are safe." She lifted the sack from his shoulder and grunted. "It weighs as much as a bison calf," she said. "How did you carry it so far?"

Volt threw up his hands. "He wastes his time going off like a medicine woman, looking for herbs and shells. Now that he has picked a mate it is time he settled down and lived with his clan."

Kala smiled. She winked at Tao and took Deha by the hand. "Come," she said, "we have rabbit stew on the fire."

After Tao ate, he slept. He awoke late in the morning, strong and refreshed but still feeling a sense of failure at having lost so much of the medicine.

As he walked toward Kala's hut, he was surprised to see her drying out the long ribbons of kelp by hanging them in the bright sunlight over the branches of the hackberry bushes. Deha sat nearby frying the shell meat on flat stones around a fire.

Tao looked at Kala, his eyes wondering. "There is enough medicine?" he asked.

"Enough to begin the healing," she said, "so we do what we can."

All day long Kala and Deha prepared the medicine. When the kelp was dried, Kala placed the leaves on a flat stone, where Deha ground them into a coarse powder. It was long, slow work, and it took many leaves to make a small amount of medicine.

After frying, the shell meat was mashed together with walnuts and acorns, shaped into small round cakes, and baked on a hearthstone.

Two days later, when some of the medicine was ready, Kala wrapped it in a skin made of bison gut and gave it to Tao. "Let Jema mix the kelp powder in birch tea," she said, "and have the sick children drink some every day. The cakes they can eat whenever they are hungry." She stood with her stout legs wide apart, wiping her hands on her skirt. "It is not nearly enough," she said, "but it is a start."

As she spoke, a group of children ran by, laughing and shouting and chasing after Ram.

"You see," said Kala, "our children play in the sun. The sick children of the mountains live in the darkness of the cave. This is not good. Besides the medicine, Jema must get them out into the sunlight."

The next morning Tao made ready to go back to the Land of the Mountain People. He was about to leave, when Deha touched him on the arm. "Here," she said, handing him three dolls, each made with sticks and straw, with tiny faces painted on dried earth apples, "give these to the children. Tell them I miss them and as soon as they are well they must come to see me."

For many days Tao stayed with Jema and the sick children. Each morning he carried the children out and sat them down on the path in front of the cave. At first they put their hands up over their faces to shield their eyes from the bright sunlight. But soon they became used to it, and they liked being out in the open, where they played with their straw dolls, drank their medicine tea, and ate their shellfish cakes.

Tao hunted along the riverbank, bringing back salmon, swan eggs, and mussels. He brought them handfuls of tasty blueberries as a treat for taking their medicine.

He watched closely, fearful that Zugor might interfere. But only once did Tao see him peering from behind the laurel bushes, a leering grin on his face. Even then he only gave his silly "Tee-hee-hee" and disappeared into the shadows. After many days the children began to gain strength. Two of them started to walk on steadier legs, and the third could now stand without help.

Every few days Tao crossed the river to go to the camp of the Valley People to get more medicine. One afternoon Kala met him in the clearing. He saw the concern in her face. "What is wrong?" he asked.

She put out her hand, holding two medicine cakes and a few pinches of kelp powder. "We have used up all the shell meat," she said.

Tao groaned. "So soon?"

"Yes," said Kala, "and this is the last of the kelp leaves."

"And without more medicine the children will not get well?" said Tao.

Kala shook her head. Her silence told him the answer.

That afternoon he walked alone to the edge of camp, where he sat under the big oak tree. The children saw him and gathered around, singing and playing, chasing one another with their willow sticks. Tao winced as he thought of the children up in the mountain cave, who were happy just to be able to walk.

He sat there mulling it over, blaming himself, when Deha came down with Ram and sat beside him. Tao was silent. "What do you think about?" she asked.

Tao shrugged. "About the medicine," he said. "Maybe I should go back to the Great Waters to get more."

"You cannot go alone," said Deha. "You will need help, someone stronger than I, someone who can carry the heavy sacks and help fight the hyenas."

"Who?" asked Tao. "Who would do it? The hunters are afraid of the spirits. Volt is interested only in the hunting. Kala and Jema are too old."

They were silent for a moment as they gazed out over the valley.

Then Deha spoke. "I was thinking," she said, "if we cannot bring the medicine to the children, why can we not bring the children to the medicine?"

Tao stood up slowly, turning the thought over in his mind. Then his eyes widened and he grinned. "You mean to the Great Waters?"

"Yes," said Deha. "When we get there, Shag and his family will help us. The children will have all the medicine they need."

"And Kala showed us how to make it," said Tao, his voice full of hope now. Once again he looked out toward the river. "I will build a new raft," he said, "stronger and wider than the first one, big enough to carry all of us and our belongings. It will take time, but by then the children should be strong enough for the long journey."

"And I can help," said Deha.

"Yes," said Tao. "While I build it I will camp down by the river. You and Ram can bring food and other things that I will need."

They talked excitedly about their new plans, when suddenly they heard a rustling in the brier bushes behind them. Tao looked around just in time to see a stooped figure disappear into the shadows.

"What is it?" asked Deha.

"Zugor, snooping again," said Tao.

"Do you think he heard?"

"It doesn't matter," said Tao. "He cannot stop us, and we will soon be far away from his threats and curses."

"I worry that he might harm the children," said Deha.

The boy shook his head. "I will build the raft in the shallows just below the little cave. Jema can keep a close watch and let me know what Zugor does."

Without waiting any longer, Tao went back to camp to gather up his hand ax, some chisels, and scrapers.

Kala watched as he tucked the flint tools under his belt. She shook her head. "Now you go running off again," she said. "Volt is right, you live like a snow goose, wherever the wind blows."

Tao smiled but went on with his preparations.

Kala stood with her fat legs apart, her hands on her hips. "What else do you need?"

"Grass rope," said Tao, "a good hammer stone, and some leather thongs."

The old woman went into her hut and came out with the items Tao had asked for. "If the rope is not long enough I can weave more," she said. "I will send Deha with some rabbit meat and chestnuts. You can still find salmon eggs down in the shallows."

It was early afternoon when Tao walked out across the plains. He made a wide swing around the piney woods and, just as he expected, he saw Tonda the rhino out in the sunlight, browsing on the scattered birch scrub with her newborn calf. Tao stopped to watch her for a moment, then went on quietly so as not to disturb her.

Down on the riverbank he cleared a spot on the sandy beach near the shallows on which to build his raft. As he had once before, he selected newly fallen pine and hickory logs lying on the forest slope. He stripped off the branches and twigs with his hand ax, tied a length of grass rope around each one, and dragged it down to the beach. There he laid the logs side by side, and bound them tightly together with leather thongs and long strings of vines and cedar roots.

He worked for three days, pounding in extra posts so the children would have something to hold on to. Finally he tied in the last log and was busy driving in the center post with his hammer stone, when he heard the shrill giggle, "Tee-hee-hee, tee-hee-hee." He looked up to see Zugor dancing along the far bank, screeching at the top of his voice. "A curse on you and the blind one," he yelled. "You go back to the Great Waters. But I think you go back without the children, maybe even without the blind one!"

Tao turned back to his work, trying to ignore the wild threats. He cannot stop us, he said to himself. When we are ready we will carry the children down to the raft and leave him on the shore, screaming and shouting. Then we will be rid of him.

Zugor kept up his annoying taunts. "Hear me, clan

boy! Before you tempt me further, beware the curse of the demons. One by one the children may die, tee-hee-hee. Or maybe you will never take them out of the cave alive, tee-hee-tee-hee."

Tao felt a cold chill run up the back of his neck. He cringed, and his mind raced ahead as he thought of what could happen. No . . . Zugor would not dare hurt the children. It would be the same as if they were cured. He would be left with no demons at all. But what if Zugor didn't care? What if he were mad enough to do it?

There was only one more day. He glanced high up over the spruce trees to the side of the mountain, where he could just make out the dark opening of the little cave, and he hoped Jema was keeping a close watch.

19

With the raft finished Tao waited only for Deha to come with Ram and the water skins. He looked down toward the valley and saw Jema coming along the path from the plains, where she had gone to collect grass for new bedding. Yet she was empty-handed and seemed to be in a hurry, hunched over, trying to run. Halfway there, she saw Tao. She stopped, cupped her hands around her mouth, and yelled, "Tao, Tao! Zugor has—"

The boy heard only that much, but from the way she acted he knew something was wrong. Vaulting on his spear, he ran to meet her.

Jema stood in the middle of the path, waiting for him, breathing hard. She pointed off across the plains. "Zugor," she said, "Zugor—" She stopped to catch her breath.

"Zugor what?"

"Zugor caught Deha coming with the water skins," she gasped.

Tao put his hand on the woman's shoulder. "It's all right," he said. "Ram will not let him hurt her."

Jema shook her head. "No, he drove Ram away with a dead polecat. Even now Zugor drags her across the plains."

"Where?"

"Near the piney woods."

Tao felt a knot in the pit of his stomach. The piney woods, Tonda's stomping grounds. Now that she had a calf, she would charge anything in sight.

He vaulted out across the plains, dodging clumps of willows, jumping over stones and fallen logs, almost stumbling in his haste. Small bands of roe deer darted away in front of him as he plunged through the waist-high grass.

He crossed a shallow stream in the middle of the plains. There he found a tall willow tree and climbed high up into its branches. He looked far out over the grasslands but saw only the grazing herds of bison and saiga antelope on the horizon.

He lifted his hand to his forehead to shield his eyes against the bright morning sun. Shimmering waves of heat rose up through the yellow grass, and high overhead a trio of vultures circled slowly in the cloudless sky. Again and again he searched, turning his gaze from one side to the other, but he saw no sign of Zugor.

He started to climb down, when, out of the corner of his eye, he saw a small band of horses galloping off in fright. And just beyond the piney woods, he could make out a man pulling a girl by the arm, dragging her through the grass, heading for the river.

Tao knew it was Deha, and he could see her tugging, fighting to get free. Tao was still too far away to hear her screams, but he winced when he saw she was getting close to the piney woods.

He jumped down from the tree and continued through the high grass, vaulting on his spear as fast as he could. He had to reach them before they got any closer, or it would be too late.

Frightened antelope stampeded out of his way as he raced on. His breath grew short and sweat poured down his face. Long before Zugor and Deha could hear him, Tao started shouting, "Go back, go back! Tonda is with calf, she will kill you!"

On and on he ran, hoping he would not be too late. He could hear Deha's voice faintly now as she struggled to get free. He saw a lone boulder standing off to one side. He ran to it, climbed on top, and stood there, panting heavily. Not far away he saw Zugor, his right hand tight around Deha's wrist, pulling her along.

Deha kicked out at him. She pummeled him on the shoulder with her fist. But she could not see, and most of her blows had little effect. "Let me go, you stupid old man! You have no say over me," she cried. "Let me go!"

In spite of his age Zugor was still strong enough to overpower her. "Quiet, girl," he shouted. "Your demons are the vile spirits of darkness. Back into the cave with you, where you belong."

Tao jumped down from the boulder and ran toward them. They could hear him now as he waved his arms and shouted, "Go back, go back! Tonda is with calf. She will kill you both if you go any closer."

Zugor ignored the warning. He kept pulling the girl behind him, straight toward the piney woods, as if he did not care.

Tao ran closer to get the old man's attention. "Tonda is with calf," he shouted again. "She will not let you pass."

At last Zugor looked at him, leering, laughing. "Tee-hee-hee," he snickered like a crazy fool. "Tonda is no danger." He held up his hand and shook his fist. "I have the magic; I have the shining stone. She can do us no harm."

Tao stopped, unable to believe what he heard. He had forgotten the shining stone. He started to walk closer, but he had taken only a few steps when he felt the ground shake. He looked up and saw Tonda coming around the edge of the piney woods. She stopped, her head straight out, sniffing the air. Her new calf came trotting right behind her.

Tonda's eyes blazed in anger. Intruders were close and she feared for her calf. She pawed the ground and snorted a deep-throated bellow.

Zugor gripped Deha's wrist with one hand and held

the shining stone over his head with the other. "Tee-hee-hee," he laughed again. "Let the beasty thing come. I will drive her off like a frightened rabbit."

Tao kept his eyes on the rhino, desperately trying to think of some way to distract her.

Deha pulled with both hands to get away. She couldn't see, but she heard the snorting beast and sensed the danger.

But Zugor stood there, grinning like a fool. He held up the shining stone, waving his arm about, shouting, daring the rhino to charge.

Tonda stared at him. She bellowed and stepped forward. Her pig tail curved up over her rump, and Tao knew she was about to charge. He moved closer to be sure she saw him and clapped his hands. She spun around in a fury of rage, snorting, unable to decide which one to attack.

Suddenly Ram dashed in from the tall grass. He snapped at Tonda's heels, worrying her, keeping her off guard.

But Zugor was determined to use the shining stone. He danced around in front of the angry rhino, pulling Deha after him. Tao watched in horror as he taunted her. "Come, beast of demons!" he yelled. "I have the magic stone. Come, kill us if you can."

Tonda snorted and made up her mind. She charged at the madman, her massive head down, her deadly horn straight out.

Once again Tao shouted and waved his arms to distract her. But it was no use. Tonda thundered on, straight for Zugor, her pounding hooves echoing across the plains, shaking the earth.

At that moment Deha broke away. She stumbled backward and fell. She picked herself up and groped around in her world of darkness, not knowing which way to run.

Zugor stood firm, his spindly legs wide apart. He held up the stone, but he held it the wrong way, with the shiny side against the palm of his hand, not catching the sunlight.

Tao groaned in realization. The old man thought it was magic. He did not know how to use it.

Tao could only stand and watch as the enraged beast charged on. With her calf right behind her, she galloped straight for Zugor, her enormous bulk looming over him.

Zugor stood firm, holding the useless stone and laughing. Tao cringed as Tonda slammed into the old man. She caught him on the end of her horn and tossed him over her back. He landed in a heap in the yellow grass. The angry beast spun around. Zugor groaned in pain and tried to get up. But it was too late. As Zugor climbed to his knees, the great beast hooked him once again. She threw him high into the air. He landed with a thud and rolled over, facedown, blood flowing from the wound in his back.

Tao saw the shining stone glinting in the grass where the old man had dropped it. He dove for it and scooped it up in his hands, then turned to face Tonda.

But she no longer saw him. Instead her tiny eyes were on Deha, still groping around, her hands out in front of her. Tao saw her tremble, and he knew the terror she must be going through as she waited in her darkness, listening to the snorting and the pounding hooves.

He dashed forward, holding up the shining stone to catch the sunlight. Tonda ignored him. Instead she charged directly at Deha. A dead swamp oak stood nearby.

Tao yelled, "Run! Run for the tree right behind you."

Deha ran, but she ran in the wrong direction, heading straight for the charging rhino.

"The other way," Tao shouted.

Deha turned quickly, running the opposite way.

Tao jumped in front of the charging beast. He held up the shining stone, flashing the sunlight in her eyes. She stopped and shook her head, then spun around and went after the girl again.

Deha tripped on a root and went down, rolling over and over, tumbling in the grass. Tonda galloped after her. Ram leaped in front of the rhino, throwing her off stride. She stopped again, grunting and snorting. She swung her head from side to side, breathing heavily.

Ram raced around her, snapping and growling, keeping her in place, giving Deha time to get to her feet.

The rhino calf caught the movement and lunged forward.

Again Tao shouted, "Run, Deha, run!"

But Deha stood in her darkness, bewildered, not knowing which way to run. The little calf galloped up behind her. He brushed against her with his shoulder, slamming her into the swamp oak.

Tao heard the dull thud as Deha's head hit the trunk. He saw her fall, then lie motionless beside it. Quickly he jumped between Deha and Tonda, flashing the sunlight again in the old rhino's eyes.

In a wild fury now, Tonda was too angry to back down. With a grunting snort she trotted closer, still shaking her head from side to side to avoid the blinding light.

Out of the corner of his eye, Tao saw Deha still lying beneath the tree. She needed help, but he could do nothing until he drove off this angry beast. He kept flashing the sunlight in Tonda's eyes as she pawed the ground and bellowed, getting ready to charge again.

Just then the calf came back. Tao saw it tremble and press against its mother's side. Almost without thinking, Tao flashed the light in the little one's eyes. It backed away, still trembling. Then with a loud squeal, it spun around and fled into the safety of the woods.

The old cow stood there for a moment, puzzled, looking for her calf. Then she too spun around and trotted back into the piney woods.

Tao ran over to where Deha lay on the ground. Ram was already there, licking her face to wake her up. At first Tao thought she was dead. Then he saw her eyes blink. Except for a bad bruise on the side of her forehead, she seemed unhurt.

Deha moaned and lifted her arm as Tao helped her to her feet. She turned her head as if looking around. With a startled cry she raised her face to the sky. She smiled a smile of endless joy and threw out her hands. "Tao! Tao! I can see!" she cried. "I can see light, and I can see shapes. Not clear, but I can see!" She pointed. "Look, there is a tree, and there a stone, and there is Ram. I can see again, I can see!" She kept saying it over and over.

It seemed like magic. Yet Tao had seen her strike her head against the tree, and he knew that in some strange way, it had given her back her sight.

They stood there for a long time as Deha looked around, enjoying the waving fields of yellow grass, the towering outlines of the trees, the movement of birds. She knelt down beside Ram, ruffling the fur around his neck and shoulders, all the while laughing and crying at the same time, "I can see, Ram, I can see again."

As if he knew, the wolf dog licked her face and whimpered softly.

Deha walked about, a bright, happy smile on her face,

taking in everything around her. Then suddenly she stopped and stared into the trampled grass. She put both hands up to her face and gasped, "It's Zugor!"

"Yes," Tao said, "the madman is dead. He tried to stop Tonda with the shining stone. He did not know the magic is in the sun, not in the stone."

20

Tao and Deha stood looking down at the scrawny old man. Tao rolled him over gently. His wrinkled face was twisted, his eyes open as if in startled surprise.

"He will make no more curses," said Tao. "He will call up no more demons."

Deha blinked and rubbed her head. "I hurt," she said, "but it is better to see." Then she looked down again at the old man. "What will we do with him?" she asked. "It is true he was mean and bad, but we should not just leave him here for the vultures."

"Maybe Jema or one of the hunters will help me carry him back to his cave," said Tao.

Deha shook her head. "No, they will not go," she said. "The clan people call it a place of death. They are afraid." She glanced up and saw a pair of vultures already circling low overhead, waiting. "I can see now, so I will help you. Besides, the old man is not heavy."

They slung the body from a long birch pole and started to carry him across the plains toward the river. Ram raced along in front of them. Halfway there they met Jema. She was standing on a boulder. She climbed down to meet them. "I saw it all," she said, breathing hard with excitement. "I saw everything." She looked at Deha as if she were seeing a ghost. She waved her hand in front of the girl's face and watched her blink. "You can see," she cried, "you can see. It is like magic." She held out her hand, and Deha touched it. Jema smiled. "Yes," she said, "you can truly see."

Then she looked down at the limp body hanging from the pole, and her dark eyes widened with fear. "Where do you take him?" she asked.

"To his cave," said Tao. "Will you show us the way?"

Jema tensed and fell back. "I will take you only part-way," she said, "then I will tell you how you might find the cave."

Tao nodded, and he and Deha carried the old man across the shallows and up through the hemlocks.

When they came to the edge of the spruce forest, Jema stopped. "Go up through the spruce wood till you come to the great black stone where the trail ends," she said. "Climb up to the second ridge and follow it toward the top of the mountain. Somewhere up there, behind a row of giant cedar trees, the hunters say the cave will surely be found."

Tao and Deha left Jema and climbed slowly up the

steep slope, hoisting the long pole on their shoulders as it bent under the dead man's weight. Thick clouds covered the sun, turning the deep woods into long caverns of dark, overhanging branches.

Ram dashed around, flushing up wood grouse, their drumming wings resounding in the shadowy silence. From high overhead they heard the *whoooo, whoooo, whoooo* of a great gray owl.

After a long climb, they reached the foot of the ridge. It towered over them, a brownish-gray cliff slanting up toward the top of the mountain. They followed it, climbing slowly along the base, their eyes searching for a dark hollow that might be a cave.

Soon the ground leveled off. Wisps of fog hung like hazy clouds, gray and gloomy, drifting low through the trees. The forest itself moaned as heavy limbs scraped against each other in the soft breeze.

Then, not far ahead, they saw the row of giant cedar trees, and at the far end appeared the yawning mouth of a dark cave.

Ram pushed his way through the laurel bushes. He lifted his head and sniffed the air as Tao and Deha followed, lugging their gruesome burden.

Clumps of waist-high ferns grew along the path leading up to the entrance, while rivulets of water trickled down the rocky walls.

All around them the decomposed skulls of bears, roe deer, hyenas, and other beasts sat upon tall stakes driven into the ground, filling the air with the foul stench of rotting flesh. Clouds of flies and bees buzzed around the opening of the cave, attracted by the reeking odor.

Then Deha gritted her teeth as she helped carry the old man past the buzzing flies and into the cave. There they lowered Zugor to the ground and waited until their eyes became accustomed to the dim light.

Tao and the girl recoiled at the signs of death all around them. The cave was even more grisly inside than out.

A huge mammoth skull covered with moss stood inside the cave. The leg, rib, and skull bones of horses, bears, and wolves lay strewn across the floor. Hideous wooden masks of animal demons with long teeth and horns hung from the walls next to a row of shabby leopard skins dangling from wooden pegs. In the nooks and crannies sat empty turtle shells and the shriveled bodies of snakes, toads, and lizards.

Tao looked around for a place to put the body. He knew he could not bury it here in the cave, so he untied the long pole and, with Deha's help, lifted up the body and draped it gently over the big mammoth skull in the center of the room.

They stood quietly for a moment, looking down at the old man. From deep inside the cave they could hear the echoing *drip, drip, drip* of water. Somehow it reminded Tao of the old man's silly laughter, *Tee-hee-hee, tee-hee-hee.* He looked down at the flat face, the heavy brow with the eyes already sinking into the sockets, and for some strange reason he felt sorry for the crazy Neander. He was tough and tenacious, two things Tao admired. And he would have made a good shaman, only, as Kala and Graybeard might say, he was foolish enough to believe in his own magic.

They left him there, with the flies already gathering around his crumpled body, and slowly and silently they made their way down the steep slope.

When Tao and Deha reached the camp, the Mountain People were milling about in the clearing, waiting for them. Jema, Wodak, and the elders crowded around Deha, plying her with questions, listening to her story, full of wonder and excitement.

Wodak approached Tao, followed by Gardo and some of the elders. "You left the old man in his cave of demons?"

"Yes," said Tao. "He will cast no more spells, make no more curses."

"Good," said Wodak. "The evil spirits are gone. Once again, we can live without fear."

The elders nodded in agreement.

Wodak spoke with them for a moment. Then he turned back to Tao and folded his arms across his chest. "First you bring life from fire," he said. "Then you cure the blindness. Now you go to heal the children." He looked at the elders again. "Is it not true?"

"It is magic," said Gardo, "true magic."

Tao shook his head in protest. "It is not I who did the healing. It was only . . ." Tao stopped without finishing his words, for he saw they were not listening. Besides, he remembered once again what Graybeard had said: "If they wish to call it magic, then let it be so."

The elders went on speaking among themselves, and Tao heard his name a number of times. Finally Wodak held up his hand for silence. "Ever since Graybeard died, we have need of a real shaman," he said. "One who will heal the sickness and help the people in their troubles. We think Tao should be the one."

Tao stiffened and felt a chill run up his spine. It was the thing he had never dared to think of. Yet now he stood here, with Wodak, Jema, and all the clan people waiting for his answer.

"I am pleased by your words," he said. "But I have much to learn before I become a shaman. First I must go with Deha and the children to the Great Waters to finish the healing. Then when I come back we will talk about being a shaman."

Tao waited by the river as Deha and Jema carried the three children down to the raft. In the two weeks used to strengthen the children for the trip, Deha's sight had been almost fully restored. What at first were just colors and shapes were now fine details, and Deha's excitement had yet to lessen. She yearned to see the Great Waters.

Many of the clan people were there to see them off. When all was ready, the two leaders, Volt and Wodak, stood side by side, while Kala and Jema waited under the big willow tree.

Tao waved good-bye and climbed aboard the raft. With his long birch pole, he pushed out from shore. He heard the parting cries of the clan people as the raft drifted slowly downstream.

The clan people heard the lilting notes of the flute as Deha played for the children.

Wodak turned to Volt. "One day your son will come home to be our shaman."

Volt smiled and shook his head. "Tao's home is everywhere. If he is to be a shaman, he will be a shaman of all the clans."

Wodak nodded. "Then truly he will follow in the footsteps of Graybeard."

Author's Note

Many writers have told stories of the Stone Age hunters of prehistoric Europe. But few have focused on the celebrated cave painters of France and Spain. Yet the hidden grottos of the Dordogne valley, the caverns of Altamira, and the Mediterranean Sea caves all tell a thousand stories of gifted lives and brave hunters, tales as daring as the *Iliad,* as romantic as *Camelot,* and as mystical as the *Arabian Nights.*

The preceding story is a humble effort to tell one of those odysseys as it might have happened fifteen to twenty thousand years ago.

The ailments of the three children in the story would today be considered a form of rickets. Although the old shaman and medicine woman did not know the reason, the magic cure would have been the rich source of minerals and vitamins in the kelp and shellfish.

The blind girl, Deha, lost her sight by striking her head as she fell from a tree. At the end of the story she regains it by another sharp blow to the head. This phenomenon has been reported several times in medical records. It has to do with a shock to the optic nerve.

The Neanders mentioned in the story are the Neanderthals, a race of early man already on the verge of extinction when the cave painters came to the mountains and valleys of what is now France and Spain. Existing in small isolated groups, they were short, robust, and rather hairy, with large square jaws and sloping brows. However, they were not the brutes or idiots they were once thought to be. They invented the club, the spear, hand axes, and the use of clothing, and they buried their dead, a hint that they may have been the first men to believe in a religion.

But they were different and were probably shunned and looked down upon by the more modern Cro-Magnon cave painters.